Translated
by
Xu Yuanchong

总要旷达

许渊冲译苏轼诗词

［宋］苏轼◎著

许渊冲◎译

U0129864

北京联合出版公司
Beijing United Publishing Co.,Ltd.

图书在版编目（ＣＩＰ）数据

总要旷达：许渊冲译苏轼诗词 /（宋）苏轼著；许渊冲译 . -- 北京：北京联合出版公司，2023.9
ISBN 978-7-5596-7124-0

Ⅰ．①总… Ⅱ．①苏… ②许… Ⅲ．①苏轼（1036-1101）－宋诗－诗歌欣赏②苏轼（1036-1101）－宋词－诗歌欣赏 Ⅳ．① I207.2

中国国家版本馆 CIP 数据核字（2023）第 122405 号

总要旷达：许渊冲译苏轼诗词

作　　者：［宋］苏轼
译　　者：许渊冲
出 版 人：赵红仕
选题统筹：邵　军
产品经理：田　硕
责任编辑：周　杨
封面设计：末末美书

北京联合出版公司出版
（北京市西城区德外大街 83 号楼 9 层　100088）
北京联合天畅文化传播公司发行
北京旺都印务有限责任公司印刷　新华书店经销
字数 200 千字　880 毫米 ×1230 毫米　1/32　10 印张
2023 年 9 月第 1 版　2023 年 9 月第 1 次印刷
ISBN 978-7-5596-7124-0
定价：49.00 元

Tune: " A RIVERSIDE TOWN"
~~DREAMING OF MY DECEASED WIFE ON THE NIGHT~~
~~OF THE 20th DAY OF THE 1st MOON~~

1075

For ten long years the living of the dead knows ~~weights~~. nought.
   Should the dead be forget
   And to mind never brought?

Her lonely grave is a thousand miles away.
To whom ~~can~~ my grief can I convey?

Revived e'en if she be, could she still know me?
   My face is worn with care
   And frosted is my hair.

I dreamed of going back to my home-town last night:
   She's making up her face
   At the window with grace.

We gazed at each other hushed,
But tears from our eyes gushed.
(Year by year my broken heart will abide)
By the pine-clad hill-side
   On a bright moon-lit night.

许渊冲译《江城子·乙卯正月二十日夜记梦》原稿

Tune: "PRELUDE TO THE MELODY OF WATER"
MID AUTUMN FESTIVAL
1076

When will the bright moon appear?
    Wine cup in hand, I ask the blue sky.
I do not know what time of year
    It would be tonight in the palace on high.

    Riding the wind, there I would fly,
But I'm afraid the crystalline palace would be
Too high and too cold for me.

I rise and dance, with my shadow I play.
On high as on earth, would it be as gay?

    The moon goes round the mansions red
    With gorgeous doors to shed
    Her light upon the sleepless bed.

She seems to have no cause to grieve.
Why does she often shine so full on us taking leave?

Men have sorrow and joy, they part or meet again;
The moon may be round or not, she may wax or wane.
There has been nothing perfect since olden days.

So, let us wish that man live as long as he can!
Though miles apart, we'll share the beauty she displays.

许渊冲译《水调歌头·明月几时有》原稿

Tune: "THE MOON ON THE WEST RIVER"
LINES WRITTEN ON A BRIDGE
1082

Wave on wave glimmers by the river shores;
    Sphere on sphere dimly appears in the sky.
Though unsaddled is my white-jade-like horse,
    Drunken, asleep in the sweet grass I'll lie.

My horse's hoofs may break, I'm afraid.   (jade.
The breeze-rippled brook paved by the moon with white
I attach my horse to a green willow
On the bridge and I pillow
My head on my arm till the cuckoo's songs awake
A spring daybreak.

Tune: "CALMING THE WAVES"
CAUGHT IN RAIN ON MY WAY TO THE SANDY LAKE
1082

Listen not to the rain beating against the trees.
I had better walk slowly while chanting at ease.
I prefer cane and sandals to a horse. For who
        Will care for you?
A straw cloak in the rain, I'll do what I like to.

Drunken, I am sobered by the vernal wind shrill
      And rather chill.
In front, I see the slanting sun atop the hill;
Turning my head, I see the dreary beaten track.
   (Shall I go back?)
(Rain or shine, I'll have my own will.)

许渊冲译《西江月·顷在黄州》《定风波·莫听穿林打叶声》原稿

At dawn I see the hills recumbent lie;
At dusk I see them towering high.
It is true these green hills are full of grace,
They try to please you by changing their face.

Extending curtain-like from east to west.
Spring comes, but where's my home with its ~~carved~~
balustrade?
If autumn is sad, then spring is much sadder still.
Sailing on the calm Lake, I long for River Brocade/
(Mount Recumbent reminds me of Eye-brow-like Hill.)
And Mount Eyebrows at sight the recumbent hill.

If a rambler looks for the place where have rambled I,
(He need but come to where Recumber Green Hills lie.)
He need but come to where green hills recumbent lie.

DRINKING AT THE LAKE FIRST IN SUNNY AND THEN
IN RAINY WEATHER
1073

The brimming waves delight the eye in sunny rays;
The dimming hills give a rare view in rainy haze.
(Like the fair West Lady the West Lake looks her best)
(Whether she be richly adorned or plainly drest.)
The West Lake looks like the fair lady at her best
Whether she is richly adorned or plainly dressed.

许渊冲译《饮湖上初晴后雨》原稿

SU SHI (1037 - 1101)
Tune : "A Riverside Town"
HUNTING AT MIZHOU

Rejuvenated, my fiery zeal I display:
    Left hand leashing a yellow hound,
On the right wrist a falcon gray.

A thousand silk-capped and sable-coated horsemen sweep
    Across the rising ground
And hillocks steep.

Townspeople come out of the gate
To watch the tiger-hunting magistrate.

Heart gladdened with strong wine, who cares
For a few frosty hairs?

When will the imperial court send
An envoy to recall the exile? Then I'll bend

My bow like a full moon, and aiming northwest, I
Will shoot down the wolf from the sky.

                              Translated on Dec. 18, 1980

Note : The poet served as magistrate of Mizhou in 1075
       and 1076. It was a poor district where officials
       under a cloud were sent. The wolf stands here
       for the Jiang tribesmen then fighting with the
       Hans.

许渊冲译《江城子·密州出猎》原稿

Tune: THE CHARM OF A MAIDEN SINGER"
REFLECTIONS ON THE ANCIENT BATTLEFIELD AT RED CLIFF
1082

The Great River eastward flows,
With its waves are gone all those
 Gallant heroes of bygone years.

 West of the ancient fortress appears
The Red Cliff where General Zhou won his early fame
When the Three Kingdoms were in flame.

Jagged rocks tower in the air,
 Swashing waves beat on the shore,
  Rolling up a thousand heaps of snow.

To match the hills and the river so fair,
 How many heroes of yore
  Made a great show!

I recall those years when Zhou Yu was at the height
Of his success, so brave and so bright,
 Newly wedded to the fair, a young lady fair.

In a silk hood, with a plume fan in hand,
(Talking and laughing, and) He laughed and talked and
 Enemy ships were destroyed like castles in the air.

I visit in fancy the ancient land,
 (Men of sentiment would laugh and say)
  Too early has my hair turned gray.

Life is but like a dream,
I would fain drink to the moon on the stream.

许渊冲译《念奴娇·赤壁怀古》原稿

目 录

凤翔：应似飞鸿踏雪泥

辛丑十一月十九日，既与子由①别于郑州西门之外，马上赋诗一篇寄之

不饮胡为醉兀兀②？

此心已逐归鞍发。

归人犹自念庭闱，

今我何以慰寂寞？

登高回首坡垅隔，

惟见乌帽出复没。

苦寒念尔衣裘薄，

独骑瘦马踏残月。

路人行歌③居人乐，

童仆怪我苦凄恻。

亦知人生要有别，

但恐岁月去飘忽。

寒灯相对记畴昔④，

夜雨何时听萧瑟？

君知此意不可忘，

慎勿苦爱高官职！

注释

①子由：苏轼弟苏辙，字子由。②兀兀：昏沉的样子。③行歌：边行走边歌唱。④畴昔：往日。

A Poem to My Brother Ziyou, Composed on Horseback after Parting with Him at the Western Gate of the Capital on the 19th Day of the 11th Lunar Month

Why do I look so drunken without drinking wine?

My heart is going back with your home-going steed.

Your thoughts turn to our parents and ancestral shrine.

How can I be consoled with the lonely life I'll lead?

Ascending a height, I look back and feel so sad

To see your black cap now appear, now disappear.

It is now biting cold and you are thinly clad,

Riding a lean nag 'neath the waning moon so drear.

Wayfarers sing abroad, people are glad at home,

My houseboy wonders why alone I'm desolate.

I know people may meet or part, settle down or roam,

But I dread to think how quickly years evaporate.

Facing a cold lamp, I relive the bygone days.

When may we listen to bleak wind on rainy night?

You know what I mean and must bear in mind always:

Don't outstay your office of which you should make light.

赏析

　　本诗写苏氏兄弟第一次远别，先写临别时心境，次写对对方身影的顾望关念，再写岁月易逝，末写对往事的回想和对未来的期盼，充分抒发了兄弟俩依依难分的衷情。[1]

―――――――――

1　刘乃昌：《宋诗三百首评注》，齐鲁书社2004年版，第82—84页。

和子由渑池①怀旧

人生到处知何似?

应似飞鸿踏雪泥。

泥上偶然留指爪,

鸿飞那复计东西!

老僧②已死成新塔,

坏壁③无由见旧题。

往日崎岖还记否?

路长人困蹇驴④嘶。

注释

　　①渑（miǎn）池：今河南渑池县。②老僧：僧人奉闲。③坏壁：奉闲僧舍。④蹇驴：跛脚的驴子。

Recalling the Old Days at Mianchi in the Same Rhymes as Ziyou's Poem

What do you think is human life like here or there?

It seems like a swan's traces on mud or on snow.

See the claw and nail prints by chance mud and snow bear.

Will the flying swan care what it has left below?

The old monk, dead, has left but a dagoba new;

The verse we wrote was gone with the wall in decay.

What I remember of the journey made with you

Is a weary long way and the lame donkey's bray.

赏析

　　苏轼赴凤翔任，途经渑池。苏辙送兄至郑州，分手回京，作《怀渑池寄子瞻兄》。苏轼因作此诗相和。此诗表达对人生来去无定的怅惘和往事旧迹的深情眷念。[1]

1　傅明伟：《中华千古名篇赏析》，中央编译出版社2006年版，第196—197页。

戏子由

宛丘①先生长如丘，
宛丘学舍小如舟。
常时低头诵经史，
忽然欠伸屋打头。
斜风吹帷雨注面，
先生不愧旁人羞。
任从饱死笑方朔，
肯为雨立求秦优②！
眼前勃谿③何足道，
处置六凿④须天游。
读书万卷不读律，
致君尧舜知无术。
劝农⑤冠盖闹如云，
送老齑⑥盐甘似蜜。
门前万事不挂眼，
头虽长低气不屈！

注释

①宛丘：陈州的别称。因为苏辙任陈州州学教授，所以戏称"宛丘
先生"。②秦优：指秦始皇的歌童旃，是个侏儒。③勃谿（xī）：争吵。
④六凿：即喜、怒、哀、乐、爱、恶六情。⑤劝农：指朝廷派遣到各地
视察农业的官吏。⑥齑（jī）：指腌菜，切碎的酱菜。

Written to Ziyou in Joke

My brother's tall as Confucius is said to be,
But his room in the schoolhouse looks like a boat small.
He bends his head while reading classics and history,
Suddenly he yawns, his head bumps against the wall.
The wind blows screens aside and raindrops into his face,
The onlookers feel sorry but he does not care.
The starving may be jeered at by well-fed men base,
He won't beg for shelter though rain drenches his hair.
He cares not for the discomforts before the eye,
If he can let his six spirits soar in the sky.
He's read ten thousand books without reading the law.
How could he serve a sovereign without a flaw!
The inspectors of agriculture come in throng,
Honey-like vegetables are given to the old.
Nothing at the door will remain in his eyes for long,
Though his head oft bends low, his spirit is still bold.

余杭别驾无功劳，

画堂五丈容旂旄①。

重楼跨空雨声远，

屋多人少风骚骚。

平生所惭今不耻，

坐对疲氓重鞭箠②。

道逢阳虎③呼与言，

心知其非口诺唯。

居高志下真何益，

气节消缩今无几。

文章小技安足程！

先生别驾旧齐名。

如今衰老俱无用，

付与时人分重轻！

注释

  ①旂旄（qí máo）：犛牛尾于杆首的旌旗，军将所建。②箠（chuí）：杖刑。③阳虎：即阳货，孔子所鄙视而不愿意与之见面的人。

Official of Hangzhou, I've done no worthy deed,

My painted hall is so large that flags can be displayed.

My mansion stands high and from noise of rain is freed,

With rooms uninhabited soughing winds invade.

I'm no longer ashamed of what I used to be,

And punish with flogging the accused before me.

I greet those I dislike when we meet on the way,

Though I know they are wrong, yet I say only "Aye".

What is the use of a high literary fame

When ebbs our moral courage and lowers our aim?

The trifling art of writing is of no avail,

You and I, while young, we attained the same renown.

We become worthless now we're decrepit and frail.

Let our contemporaries play us up or down!

赏析

　　本诗前六句写苏辙生活清苦，接着十句称赞苏辙，再接十句自嘲，最后四句发泄对达官贵人的鄙视之情。全诗用喜剧的手法谱写悲愤之曲，显示了苏诗"嬉笑怒骂，皆成文章"的特色。[1]

1　曾枣庄、曾弢：《苏轼诗文词选译》，凤凰出版社2017年版，第17—21页。

和子由踏青

东风陌上惊微尘，
游人初乐岁华新①。

人闲正好路旁饮，
麦短未怕游车轮。

城中居人厌城郭，
喧阗②晓出空四邻。

歌鼓惊山草木动，
箪瓢散野乌鸢③驯。

何人聚众称道人？
遮道卖符色怒嗔④。

宜蚕使汝茧如瓮，
宜畜使汝羊如麇⑤。

路人未必信此语，
强为买服禳⑥新春。

道人得钱径沽酒，
醉倒自谓吾符神！

注释

①岁华新：新年伊始。②喧阗（tián）：喧嚣嘈杂。③乌鸢（yuān）：鹰类猛禽。④色怒嗔（chēn）：面带怒色。⑤麇（jūn）：古书里指獐子。⑥禳（ráng）：祈福消灾。

Rhyming with Ziyou's "Treading the Green"

The east wind raises a fine dust on the pathways,
Excursionists are glad to enjoy new year's pleasure.
People may drink by the roadside as they have leisure,
Short wheat are not afraid of the wheels of the chaise.
Townsfolk are tired of living within city wall,
They make much noise on leaving their house in the morn.
Songs and drums jar the hills and shake trees, grass and thorn;
Picnic baskets invite tame birds, crows, kites and all.
Who is there drawing round a crowd, barring the ways?
It is a Taoist priest who sells his charms and says:
"Buy my charms and your cocoon will sure grow as big
As a jar and your sheep as a pig."
Passers-by may not believe in his words so fine,
They buy charms anyway to consecrate the spring.
The priest gets money and goes to a shop of wine,
Drunken, he boasts his charms are wonder-working thing.

赏析

　　本诗描写了苏轼回忆青少年时在家乡新春之际，人们倾城出郊游春踏青的盛况，具有浓郁的乡情。[1]

1　　陈衍选编：《宋诗精华录全译（上）（修订版）》，贵州人民出版社2009年版，第360页。

十二月十四日夜微雪，明日早往南溪小酌至晚

南溪得雪真无价，
走马来看及①未消。
独自披榛②寻履迹，
最先犯晓③过朱桥。
谁怜屋破眠无处？
坐觉村饥语不嚣。
惟有暮鸦知客意，
惊飞千片落寒条。

注释

  ①及：趁着。②榛：杂乱的草木。③犯晓：打破清晨的寂静。

It Snowed on the Night of the 14th Day of the 12th Lunar Month. I Went to the Southern Valley on the Next Morning and Drank There Till Dusk

The snow in Southern Valley is priceless indeed,
I come there on horseback before it melts away.
Alone, I follow the trail in a cloak of reed,
First to cross the ochre bridge at the break of day.
Who pities the homeless who have nowhere to sleep?
I find villagers hungry whose voices are low.
Only the crows at dusk know why I'm thinking deep,
Startled, they fly and shed a thousand flakes of snow.

赏析

　　嘉祐八年十二月十四日晚，下了当年冬天的第一场雪。于是，苏轼携一壶老酒，对着这纯洁的世界庆贺一番。

腊日①游孤山②访惠勤惠思二僧

天欲雪，

云满湖，

楼台明灭山有无。

水清出石鱼可数，

林深无人鸟相呼。

腊日不归对妻孥，

名寻道人实自娱。

道人之居在何许？

宝云山③前路盘纡。

孤山孤绝谁肯庐，

道人有道山不孤。

注释

①腊日：说法不一，有说是十二月一日，也有说是十二月八日。

②孤山：在杭州西湖。③宝云山：在西湖北面，有宝云寺。

Visiting in Winter the Two Learned Monks in the Lonely Hill

It seems that snow will fall
On a cloud-covered lake,
Hills loom and fade, towers appear and disappear.
Fish can be count'd among the rocks in water clear;
Birds call back and forth in the deep woods men forsake.
I cannot go home on this lonely winter day,
So I visit the monks to while my time away.
Who can show me the way which leads to their door-sill?
Follow the winding path to the foot of the hill.
The Lonely Hill is so lonesome. Who will dwell there?
Strong in faith, there's no loneliness but they can bear.

纸窗竹屋深自暖，

拥褐坐睡依团蒲。

天寒路远愁仆夫，

整驾催归及未晡①。

出山回望云木合，

但见野鹘②盘浮图。

兹游淡薄欢有馀，

到家恍③如梦蘧蘧④。

作诗火急追亡逋⑤，

清景一失后难摹。

注释

　　①晡（bū）：申时，黄昏之前。②野鹘（hú）：属鸷鸟类。③恍（huǎng）：恍惚。④蘧（qú）：惊动的样子。⑤亡逋（bū）：逃亡者。

Paper windows keep them warm in bamboo cottage deep;

Sitting in their coarse robes, on round rush mats they sleep.

My lackeys grumble at cold weather and long road,

They hurry me to go before dusk to my abode.

Leaving the hill, I look back and see woods and cloud

Mingled and wild birds circling the pagoda proud.

This trip has not tired me but left an aftertaste,

Come back, I seem to see in dreams the scene retraced.

I hasten to write down in verse what I saw then,

For the scene lost to sight can't be revived again.

赏析

　　这首诗分入山和出山两个片段来写，描绘了孤山幽旷的景色，写出了僧人淡泊的生活，揭示了僧人高尚的品德，意境优美，情景交融。[1]

1　陈迩冬：《苏东坡诗词选》，人民文学出版社1982年版，第15—16页。

除夜直都厅，囚系皆满，日暮不得返舍，因题一诗于壁

除日当早归，

官事乃见留。

执笔对之泣，

哀此系中囚：

小人营糇粮^①，

堕网^②不知羞。

我亦恋薄禄，

因循失归休。

不须论贤愚，

均是为食谋。

谁能暂纵遣？

闵默^③愧前修^④。

注释

　　①糇（hóu）粮：干粮，这里"糇粮"借指生活必需。②堕网：堕入法网，即犯法。③闵默：亦作悯默，心中有忧说不出来的意思。④前修：先贤。

Seeing Prisoners on New Year's Eve

I should go back early on New Year's Eve,
But my official duty detains me.
Holding my writing brush in hand, I grieve
For I am like these prisoners I see.
They cannot earn an honest livelihood,
And feel no shame at committing a crime.
I won't resign my office which I should,
And get into a rut and lose my time.
Don't ask who is foolish or who is wise.
All of us alike must scheme for a meal.
Who can be carefree from his fall and rise?
Silent before the sage, what shame I feel!

赏析

  本诗为苏轼初到杭州的除夕夜所作。除夕夜加班审判犯人，理应郁闷难当，但他却出人意料地站在人性的角度来思考问题。这是本诗的闪光之处，也是苏轼品格的耀眼之处。

别岁

故人适千里，
临别尚迟迟。
人行犹可复，
岁行那可追。
问岁安所之？
远在天一涯。
已逐东流水，
赴海归无时。
东邻酒初熟，
西舍彘^①亦肥。
且为一日欢，
慰此穷年悲。
勿嗟旧岁别，
行与新岁辞。
去去勿回顾，
还君老与衰。

注释

　①彘（zhì）：猪。

20

Farewell to the Old Year

When an old friend is to go far away,
Long, long will he linger before he parts.
Though gone away, he may come back some day.
Where can we find the old year once it departs?
May I ask whither the old year has passed?
At the end of the earth it leaves no track.
It is gone with the water flowing fast
To the East Sea and will never come back.
Wine is warmed by our neighbors on the east
And the pork of those on the west is fat.
I'd like to have one happy day at least
So that the lean year may not be grieved at.
Do not sigh for the departing old year!
Soon we shall say goodbye to New Year's Day.
Do not look back but let them disappear.
Man will grow old and his powers decay.

赏析

  本诗从"别"字着眼，十六句，四句一节。第一节用故人之别引出别岁来。第二节把与岁月之别写得感慨深沉。第三节正面写别岁欢饮的场面。最后一节，逼入一步，使感慨更加深沉。[1]

---

1 缪钺等：《宋诗鉴赏辞典》，上海辞书出版社1987年版，第326页。

守岁

欲知垂尽①岁，

有似赴壑蛇。

修鳞②半已没，

去意谁能遮？

况欲系其尾，

虽勤知奈何！

儿童强不睡，

相守夜讙③哗。

晨鸡且勿唱，

更鼓畏添挝④。

坐久灯烬落，

起看北斗斜⑤。

明年岂无年，

心事恐蹉跎。

努力尽今夕，

少年犹可夸。

注释

　　①垂尽：快要结束。②修鳞：长蛇的身躯。③讙（huān）：同"欢"。
④挝（zhuā）：敲打，此处指更鼓声。⑤北斗斜：谓时已夜半。

Staying up All Night on New Year's Eve

The end of the year is drawing near
As a snake crawls back to its hole.
We see half its body disappear
And soon we'll lose sight of the whole.
If we try to tie down its tail,
We can't succeed whate'er we do.
Children will stay up and regale
Themselves with feast the whole night through.
Cocks, wake not the dawn with your song;
Drums, do not boom out the hour now!
The wick is burned as I sit long,
I rise to see the slanting Plough.
Will there be no New Year's Eve next year?
I am afraid time waits for none.
Let us enjoy tonight with cheer
So that childhood will longer run.

赏析

  本诗细致描述了人们守岁的情景与心情。作者用形象的蛇蜕皮喻时间不可留，暗示要自始至终抓紧时间做事，免得时间过半，虽勤也难补于事。[1]

---

1 缪钺等：《宋诗鉴赏辞典》，上海辞书出版社1987年版，第326页。

春夜

春宵一刻值千金，
花有清香月有阴①。
歌管②楼台声细细，
秋千院落夜沉沉。

注释

①月有阴：月光投在花下的朦胧阴影。②歌管：歌声和管乐声。

Spring Night

A moment of spring night is worth its length of gold,

When flowers spread on moonlight and shade fragrance cold.

The slender flute from the bower plays music slender;

The tender night on garden swing casts shadow tender.

赏析

　　本诗以清新的笔触描写了春夜里迷人的景色。诗句华美而含蓄，耐人寻味。特别是"春宵一刻值千金"，成了千古传诵的名句，后来人们常常用来形容良辰美景的短暂和宝贵。[1]

1　王宝麟等：《千家诗鉴赏辞典》，商务印书馆国际有限公司2019年版，第5—7页。

石鼻城①

平时战国今无在，
陌上征夫自不闲。
北客初来试新险，
蜀人从此送残山。
独穿暗月朦胧里，
愁渡奔河苍茫间。
渐入西南风景变：
道旁修竹水潺潺。

注释

①石鼻城：即宝鸡东北30里的武城镇，相传为诸葛亮所筑。

北宋范中
立谿山行旅
圖

宋 范寬 谿山行旅圖軸 台北故宮博物院藏

宋　郭熙　秋山行旅图轴　台北故宫博物院藏

The Stone-nose Town

Where are the belligerent states of bygone days?
Wayfarers are trudging on their way without cheer.
New-come Northerners on the peril fix their gaze;
The mountaineers part with their last steep mountain here.
Alone, I make my way dimly lit by moonlight;
Saddened, I cross the river shrouded in the haze.
The Southwest land affords a quite different sight:
The ripples whisper with roadside bamboo they graze.

赏析

宋治平元年，苏轼与章敦等人游石鼻写此诗。本诗以景作结，寓情于景，含蓄表达出经过艰辛跋涉后超然物外的人生态度。

虞姬墓

帐下佳人拭泪痕，

门前壮士气如云。

仓黄不负君王^①意，

只有虞姬与郑君^②。

注释

　　①君王：指项籍。②郑君：即郑荣，这里指不负项籍的人。

Lady Yu's Tomb

In the tent fair ladies wiped away their tears;
At the door brave men gathered like a mass of cloud.
Who justified the king's trust in critical years?
Of Lady Yu and General Zheng he could be proud.

赏析

　　虞姬墓，在安徽定远县南六十里。本诗为苏轼于熙宁四年赴杭州途中过濠州时所作。诗人在虞姬墓前，感怀古人古事，赞颂了虞姬和郑荣的坚贞，颇有弦外之音。

游金山寺①

我家江水初发源，

宦游直送江入海。

闻道潮头一丈高，

天寒尚有沙痕在。

中泠②南畔石盘陀③，

古来出没随涛波。

试登绝顶望乡国，

江南江北青山多。

羁愁畏晚寻归楫④，

山僧苦留看落日。

微风万顷靴文细，

断霞半空鱼尾赤。

注释

①金山寺：在今江苏镇江西北的长江边的金山上。②中泠：泉名，在金山西。③石盘陀：形容石块巨大。④归楫：从金山回去的船。

Visiting the Temple of Golden Hill

My native town lies where the River takes its source,
As official I go downstream to the seaside.
'Tis said white-crested waves rise ten feet high at full tide,
On this cold day the sand bears traces of their force.
There stands a massive boulder south of Central Fountain,
Emerging or submerged as the tides fall or rise.
I climb atop to see where my native town lies,
But find by riverside green mountain on green mountain.
Home-sick, I will go back by boat lest I be late,
But the monk begs me to stay and view the setting sun.
The breeze ripples the water and fine webs are spun;
Rosy clouds in mid-air like fish-tails undulate.

是时江月初生魄①，

二更月落天深黑。

江心似有炬火明，

飞焰照山栖乌惊。

怅然归卧心莫识，

非鬼非人竟何物。

江山如此不归山，

江神见怪警我顽。

我谢②江神岂得已，

有田不归如江水③！

注释

①初生魄：新月初生。②谢：告诉。③如江水：古人发誓的一种方式。

Then the moon on the river sheds her new-born light,

By second watch she sinks into the darkened skies.

From the heart of the river a torch seems to rise,

Its flames light up the mountains and the crows take flight.

Bewildered, I come back and go to bed, lost in thought:

It's not a work of man or ghost. Then what is it?

It must be the River God's warning for me to quit

And go to my home-town, which I can't set at nought.

Thanking the God, I say I'm reluctant to stay,

If I won't go home, like these waves I'll pass away!

赏析

　　本诗从寄宿漫游写到金山登顶，从断霞半空写到二更月落，从江火通亮写到怅然归卧，从江神见怪写到指水为誓，或实，或虚，或看，或想，从无生有，如图如画，真是神笔巧夺天工。[1]

1　缪钺等：《宋诗鉴赏辞典》，上海辞书出版社1987年版，第330页。

自金山放船至焦山①

金山楼观何眈眈，

撞钟击鼓闻淮南②。

焦山何有有修竹，

采薪汲水僧两三。

云霾浪打人迹绝，

时有沙户③祈春蚕。

我来金山更留宿，

而此不到心怀惭。

同游兴尽决独往，

赋命④穷薄轻江潭。

清晨无风浪自涌，

中流歌啸倚半酣。

注释

　　①焦山：在长江中。②淮南：指扬州。③沙户：沙洲上的人家。
④赋命：天生的命运。

Boating from the Golden Hill to the Hermit's Hill

How gaudy does the Temple of Golden Hill glare!
To Huainan spread its beating drum and ringing bell.
What has the Hermit's Hill but bamboo here and there
And two or three monks drawing water from the well?
On its deserted shore veiled in dim mist waves beat,
Only to seek silk-worms in spring will peasants come.
In Golden Hill I stayed o'ernight to rest my feet.
Without seeing Hermit's Hill, how sorry I'd become!
My companions were disinclined to come with me.
Disfavored man alone of whirlpool risk make light.
Waves surge although the morning of the wind is free,
Half drunken, I sing in mid-stream with sweet delight.

老僧下山惊客至，

迎笑喜作巴人谈。

自言久客忘乡井，

只有弥勒为同龛。

困眠得就纸帐暖，

饱食未厌山蔬甘。

山林饥卧古亦有，

无田不退宁非贪？

展禽①虽未三见黜，

叔夜②自知七不堪。

行当投劾③谢簪组，

为我佳处留茅庵。

注释

①展禽：春秋时鲁国大夫。②叔夜：即嵇康，字叔夜。③投劾（hé）：指自劾。

The old monk comes downhill, surprised to see a guest,
And glad to greet his compatriot with a smile.
He says he has forgotten his home-town in the west,
Living together with Maitreya on this isle.
He sleeps in a warm paper curtain when tired and cold;
Hungry, he likes to eat mountain vegetables sweet.
The mountaineers have suffered hunger since days old;
Not greedy, the landless should make good their retreat.
Although I have not been dismissed from office thrice,
Yet I know there are seven things I cannot bear.
Soon I will resign for I am not free from vice,
I wish to live in thatched temple free from care.

赏析

　　本诗篇首用金山寺的香火之盛对比写出焦山的清静冷落，然后写到饮酒歌啸的超然之乐，又写到焦山老僧简朴宁静的生活，篇末表露出诗人想要辞官归隐的意愿。[1]

1　陈迩冬：《苏东坡诗词选》，人民文学出版社1982年版，第13—15页。

杭州：欲把西湖比西子

雨中游天竺灵感观音院^①

蚕欲老，

麦半黄，

前山后山雨浪浪。

农夫辍耒^②女废筐，

白衣仙人^③在高堂。

注释

　　①灵感观音院：在杭州上天竺。②辍耒（lěi）：停止农作。③白衣仙人：即观音。这里暗指官吏。

Visiting the Temple of the Compassionate God of Mercy on a Rainy Day

Silkworms grow old,

Wheat turns half gold.

On both sides of the hill the rain is pouring its fill.

Women can't weave baskets nor can men till the ground,

But high in the hall sits the immortal white-gowned.

赏析

　　本诗借讽刺观音菩萨来讽刺在其位而不谋其职的官僚，词情含蓄而强劲，语言通俗流畅，音韵和谐，具有鲜明的民歌风味。[1]

1　缪钺等：《宋诗鉴赏辞典》，上海辞书出版社1987年版，第337页。

有美堂①暴雨

游人脚底一声雷，

满座顽云②拨不开。

天外黑风吹海立，

浙东飞雨过江来。

十分潋滟金樽凸，

千杖敲铿③羯鼓催。

唤起谪仙泉洒面，

倒倾鲛室④泻琼瑰。

注释

　　①有美堂：位于杭州吴山。②顽云：浓云。③敲铿（kēng）：啄木鸟啄木声，这里借指打鼓声。④鲛室：神话中鲛人所居之处，这里指海。

Tempest at the Scenic Hall

Sight-seers hear from below a sudden thunder roars;

A skyful of storm-clouds cannot be dissipated.

The dark wind from on high raises a sea agitated;

The flying rain from the east crosses river shores.

Like wine o'erflowing golden cup full to the brim

And thousands of sticks beating the drum of sheepskin.

Heaven pours water on the poet's face and chin

That he might write with dragon's scales and pearls a hymn.

赏析

　　本诗生动地展现暴雨由远而近、横跨大江、呼啸奔来的壮观景象。首联写雨前一刹那的气氛。颔联三句是想象，四句是亲见。颈联二句具体写暴雨。尾联写观感，联想到李白的故事。[1]

1　李梦生：《宋诗三百首全解》，复旦大学出版社2007年版，第100—101页。

六月二十七日望湖楼醉书五首选三

一

黑云翻墨未遮山，

白雨跳珠乱入船。

卷地风来忽吹散，

望湖楼下水如天。

二

放生鱼鳖逐人来，

无主荷花到处开。

水枕①能令山俯仰，

风船解与月徘徊。

三

未成小隐②聊中隐，

可得长闲胜暂闲。

我本无家更安往？

故乡无此好湖山。

注释

　　①水枕：水面上的枕席。②小隐：隐居山林。

Written While Drunken in the Lake View Pavilion on the 27th Day of the 6th Lunar Month

I

Like spilt ink dark clouds spread o'er the hills as a pall;
Like bouncing pearls the raindrops in the boat run riot.
A sudden rolling gale comes and dispels them all,
Below Lake View Pavilion sky-mirrored water's quiet.

II

Captive fish and turtles set free swim after men,
Here and there in full bloom are lotuses unowned.
Pillowed on the waves, we see hills rise now, fall then;
Boating in the wind, the moon seems to whirl around.

III

Not yet secluded, in official life I seek pleasure;
Free for some time, I long to enjoy longer leisure.
Homeless as I might have been, where may I go then? Where?
The lakes and hills in my home-town are not so fair.

赏析

　　此三首为苏轼谪居杭州期间创作的组诗。第一首描绘了西湖的美丽雨景；第二首表现在船上泛游的情趣；第五首反用古诗句意，体现了一种淡然与豁达之情。[1]

1　缪钺等：《宋诗鉴赏辞典》，上海辞书出版社1987年版，第337—339页。

饮湖上初晴后雨二首选一

水光潋滟①晴方好，

山色空濛②雨亦奇。

欲把西湖比西子：

淡妆浓抹总相宜。

注释

①潋滟：水面波光闪动的样子。②空濛：迷濛缥缈的样子。

Drinking at the Lake
First in Sunny and then in Rainy Weather

The brimming waves delight the eye on sunny days;
The dimming hills give a rare view in rainy haze.
The West Lake looks like the fair lady at her best;
Whether she is richly adorned or plainly dressed.

赏析

　　本诗对西湖的特点作了极其准确而又精到的艺术概括；此外还赋予西湖以人的生命，使西湖成为美的化身，对西湖进行美的升华。因此，在难以计数的歌咏西湖的诗歌中，这首诗成为流传最广的名篇。[1]

1　缪钺等：《宋诗鉴赏辞典》，上海辞书出版社1987年版，第348—349页。

新城道中二首选一

东风知我欲山行，

吹断檐间积雨声。

岭上晴云披絮帽①，

树头初日挂铜钲②。

野桃含笑竹篱短，

溪柳自摇沙水清。

西崦③人家应最乐，

煮芹烧笋饷④春耕。

注释

①絮帽：棉帽。②钲（zhēng）：古代铜制乐器。③西崦（yān）：泛指山。
④饷：用食物款待别人。

On My Way to New Town

The eastern wind foresees I will go to the wood;
It blows off endless songs sung by rain on the eaves.
The mountain's crowned with rainbow cloud like silken hood;
The rising sun like a brass gong hangs o'er the leaves.
Peach blossoms smile o'er the bamboo fence not tall;
Willow trees by the clear sand-paved brook sway and swing.
Folks in the Western Hills should be happiest of all;
They send well-cooked food to those who till in spring.

赏析

　　本诗是苏轼在去往新城途中，对秀丽明媚的春光，繁忙的春耕景象的描绘。该诗主要写景，景中含情，反映了作者当时欢乐的心情，也表现了他厌恶俗务、热爱自然的情趣。[1]

1　缪钺等：《宋诗鉴赏辞典》，上海辞书出版社1987年版，第347—348页。

望海楼^①晚景五首选三

一

海上涛头一线来，

楼前指顾^②雪成堆。

从今潮上君须上，

更看银山二十回。

二

横风吹雨入楼斜，

壮观应须好句夸。

雨过潮平江海碧，

电光时掣紫金蛇^③。

三

青山断处塔层层，

隔岸人家唤欲麿^④。

江上秋风晚来急，

为传钟鼓列西兴。

注释

①望海楼：即中和堂东楼，在杭州凤凰山上。②指顾：指点顾盼之间，比喻时间很短。③紫金蛇：形容闪电的形状和色彩。④麿（yīng）：同"应"。

Evening Views from the Seaside Pavilion

I

The rising tide comes in from the sea in a row,

Below the Pavilion in a twinkling heaps up snow.

From now on you should come with the coming tidal bore

And you can see silver mountains twenty times more.

II

The wind blows rain into the Pavilion slant-wise,

Fine verse should be composed in praise of the grand view.

After the rain the sea turns green, no tide will rise,

The lightening flashes like a snake of golden hue.

III

Where blue hills sever, there stands a pagoda tall,

People on either shore answer each other's call.

The strong wind in an autumn evening will bring

The sound of ringing bells and beating drums to Xixing.

赏析

　　此三首为苏轼观钱塘晚潮而创作的组诗。全诗用雪堆、银山、金蛇、青山、秋风等意象来描绘钱塘晚潮及海天闪电等江景，文字如行云流水般流畅，显示了作者高超的艺术功力。[1]

1　缪钺等：《宋诗鉴赏辞典》，上海辞书出版社1987年版，第340—341页。

八月十五日看潮五绝

一

定知玉兔十分圆，
已作霜风九月寒。
寄语重门休上钥，
夜潮留向月中看。

二

万人鼓噪慑吴侬，
犹是浮江老阿童。
欲识潮头高几许，
越山浑在浪花中。

三

江边身世两悠悠，
久与沧波共白头。
造物亦知人易老，
故教江水向西流。

Watching the Tidal Bore on Mid-autumn Festival

I

The moon with jade-rabbit must be full to behold,
As in ninth month, the wind is blowing frosty cold.
Tell the Moon Goddess not to lock her door tonight,
'Tis best to watch the tidal bore in the moonlight.

II

The Southerners are scared at ten thousand men's roar
As if downstream came conquerors' warships and glaives.
If you want to know how high is the tidal bore,
See the Southern hills mingle with white-crested waves.

III

As water's flowing east, life is passing away,
Long since man has white hair and waves have their white crest.
The Creator fears lest our hair should too soon turn gray,
He orders the river to flow back to the west.

四

吴儿生长狎①涛渊，

冒利轻生不自怜。

东海若知明主意，

应教斥卤②变桑田。

五

江神河伯两醯鸡③，

海若④东来气吐霓。

安得夫差水犀手，

三千强弩射潮低！

注释

　　①狎（xiá）：玩弄。②斥卤：海边盐咸地。③醯（xī）鸡：小虫名。
④海若：海神。

IV

The Southerners from birth are fond of playing with waves,

They make light of their lives for profits and for gains.

If the East Sea knew what our sage sovereign craves,

The salt water would change into ricefields and plains.

V

The two Gods of the River vie to raise the tide,

From the westward-rolling billows rainbows will spout.

Where could we find three thousand Wu archers to chide

The billows with arrows so that the tide flow out?

赏析

　　第一首写苏轼去看钱塘江潮的打算，第二首描绘所看到的潮水的威势，第三首抒写看潮后兴起的感慨，第四首以地方官的身份抒发因看潮而生的议论，第五首再次抒发观潮所得的感想。全诗淋漓恣肆，不落常轨，体现出苏诗英爽豪迈的风格。[1]

1　唐圭璋等：《唐宋词鉴赏辞典（唐·五代·北宋）》，上海辞书出版社1988年版，第355—359页。

催试官考较①戏作

八月十五夜，

月色随处好。

不择茅檐与市楼，

况我官居似蓬岛。

凤味堂②前野橘香，

剑潭桥畔秋荷老。

八月十八潮，

壮观天下无。

鲲鹏水击三千里，

组练③长驱十万夫。

红旗青盖互明灭，

黑沙白浪相吞屠。

人生会合古难必，

此景此行那两得！

愿君闻此添蜡烛，

门外白袍④如立鹄⑤。

注释

　　①考较：指试后的阅卷、评定。②凤味（zhòu）堂：在杭州凤凰山下。
③组练：指军队。④白袍：指未仕的士子。⑤立鹄（hú）：形容伸着脖子、
踮脚盼望的样子。

Written to Examiners in Joke

On the mid-autumn night
Everywhere the moon is bright,
Over the thatched roof, over the city hall,
Over my mansion which looks like a fairy-land,
O'er the Sword Pool where lotus blooms grow old in the fall,
O'er the Phoenix Beak where wild oranges fragrant stand.
On the eighteenth of the eighth moon,
Incomparable high tide at noon:
Like water spouted three thousand miles high by whales
Or the march of ten myriads of armored men.
Red flags and blue canopies furl and unfurl like sails;
Black sand and white waves swallow each other now and then.
'Tis hard for men to get together as of old,
Candidates would regret not to see such a scene.
I hope you will burn more candles as you are told,
For outdoors candidates craning their necks can be seen.

赏析

　　本诗写月色，抓住了月色的柔美、多情；写大潮则用"鲲鹏水击""组练长驱"之喻突出其壮美、雄强，使人身临其境，感同身受。[1]

————————————

1　陈迩冬：《苏东坡诗词选》，人民文学出版社1982年版，第22—23页。

法惠寺①横翠阁

朝见吴山②横，

暮见吴山纵。

吴山故多态，

转折为君容。

幽人起朱阁，

空洞更无物。

惟有千步冈③，

东西作帘额。

春来故国归无期，

人言秋悲春更悲。

已泛平湖④思濯锦⑤，

更看横翠忆峨眉。

雕栏能得几时好，

不独凭栏人易老。

百年兴废更堪哀，

悬知⑥草莽化池台。

游人寻我旧游处，

但觅吴山横处来。

注释

①法惠寺：在杭州清波门外，旧名兴庆寺。②吴山：在今杭州市西南。③千步冈：指吴山。④平湖：指西湖。⑤濯（zhuó）锦：指成都锦江。⑥悬知：预先知道。

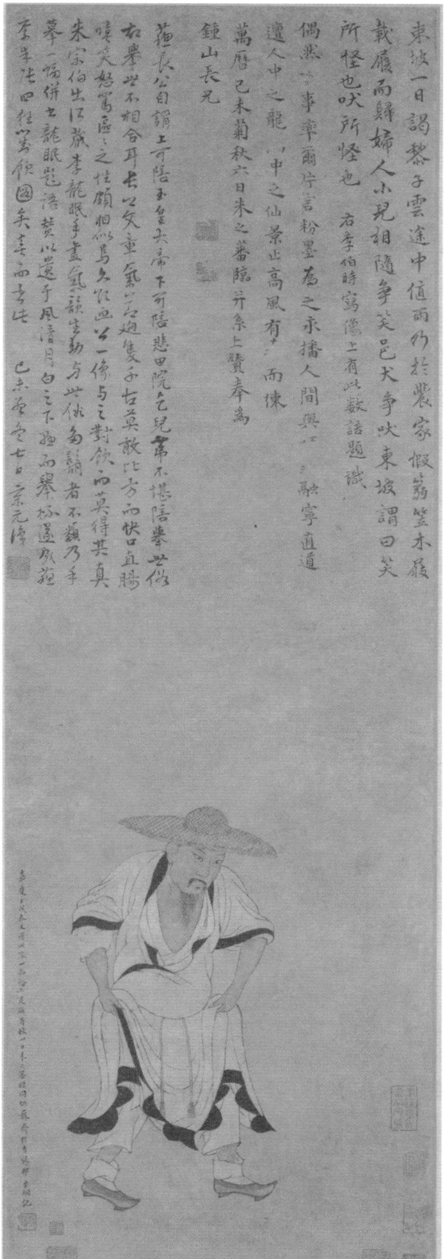

明 朱之蕃 临苏轼像轴 故宫博物院提供

宋　梁楷　东篱高士图轴　台北故宫博物院藏

The Recumbent Green Pavilion of Fahui Temple

At dawn I see the hills recumbent lie;

At dusk I see them towering high.

It is true these green hills are full of grace,

Trying to please you by changing their face.

A recluse has built a pavilion here,

With nothing round but solitude far and near

And this ridge with its thousand-pace-high crest

Extending curtain-like from east to west.

Spring comes but brings for me not a home-coming dream;

If autumn is sad, then spring is much sadder still.

On the lake I recall the Brocade-washing Stream;

And of Mount Brows reminds me the recumbent hill.

How long can the carved railings be good to behold?

The man who leans on them will easily grow old.

More lamentable is dynastic rise and fall!

We can foretell briers will grow in this painted hall.

If a rambler looks for the place where have rambled I,

He'll but find the recumbent hills before his eye.

赏析

　　这是首典型的登临诗，分为二层，即登临所见和登临所感。本诗以五言写景，七言抒情，起首四句又杂以民歌体，活泼跳荡，用韵平仄交合，寓以变化。[1]

1　缪钺等：《宋诗鉴赏辞典》，上海辞书出版社1987年版，第345—347页。

冬至日独游吉祥寺①

井底微阳回未回，

萧萧寒雨湿枯荄②。

何人更似苏夫子：

不是花时肯独来。

注释

①吉祥寺：即杭州广福寺。②荄（gāi）：草根。

Visiting Alone the Temple of Auspicious Fortune on Winter Solstice

In the depth of the well warmth has not yet come back,
Showers of cold rain have wetted withered grass root.
No one would come to visit the Temple for there lack
Flowers in full bloom, but alone I come on foot.

赏析

　　本诗写苏轼冬至独游吉祥寺的感触。吉祥寺以牡丹闻名，当牡丹盛开时，文人公卿都来游赏吟咏。诗人明咏世人对牡丹的态度，暗讽趋炎附势的世态人情。全诗在率意落笔中表达出一种清雅自赏的风致，寓意颇深。[1]

1　王远国，佘克勤：《中华传统节日诗赏析》，华中理工大学出版社1996年版，第350页。

书双竹①湛师房

暮鼓朝钟自击撞，

闭门孤枕对残釭②。

白灰旋拨通红火，

卧听萧萧雪打窗。

注释

　　①双竹：即杭州的广严寺。②釭：灯，一作"缸"。

Written for the Meditation Room of the Abbot of the Double Bamboo Monastery

You beat your evening drum and ring your morning bell,

Doors closed, a pillow facing a lamp, you rest well.

After poking among gray ashes embers red,

You hear snow-flakes fall shower by shower while abed.

赏析

　　本诗抒写苏轼夜宿寺院的心境。全诗承转清晰，相生相悖，从表面的羡佛中透露出痛苦矛盾而又迷茫无依的复杂心绪。[1]

1　唐圭璋等：《唐宋词鉴赏辞典（唐·五代·北宋）》，上海辞书出版社1988年版，第361—362页。

吴中田妇叹

今年粳^①稻熟苦迟，
庶见霜风来几时。
霜风来时雨如泻，
杷^②头出菌镰生衣。
眼枯泪尽雨不尽，
忍见黄穗卧青泥！
茅苫^③一月陇上宿，
天晴获稻随车归。
汗流肩赪^④载入市，
价贱乞与如糠粞^⑤。
卖牛纳税拆屋炊，
虑浅不及明年饥。
官今要钱不要米，
西北万里招羌儿。
龚黄^⑥满朝人更苦，
不如却作河伯妇！

注释

①粳（jīng）：俗称"大米"。②杷（pá）：同"耙"，翻土的农具。
③茅苫（shān）：茅棚。④赪（chēng）：红色。⑤粞（xī）：碎米。⑥龚黄：
龚遂、黄霸，汉代清官。这里作反语。

Lament of a Peasant Woman Living in the South of the River

To our sorrow the rice ripens so late this year,
And soon we will see the frosty autumn wind blow.
Before the frosty wind the rain pours far and near,
The sickles rust and on the rake's teeth mold will grow.
Can we bear to see golden stalks flat in mud deep?
Though we weep our eyes dry, yet the rain never stops.
In a straw shelter by the fields one month we sleep,
Once it clears, our cart comes back loaded with our crops.
Sweaty, we carry them on our shoulders chafed red
To the market where at the price of chaff they're sold.
To pay the tax we sell the ox and pull down the shed
For fuel and next year's hunger can be foretold.
In cash instead of in kind the tax should be paid
So that tribesmen be bought o'er on northwest frontier.
The peasants suffer more for wise reforms just made,
They would rather be drowned than live in such a year.

赏析

　　诗在江南秋雨成灾的背景下创作而成。全诗分为两大段，前八句为第一大段，写雨灾造成的苦难，后八句为第二大段，写虐政害民更甚于秋涝。这首诗叙事抒情，间用议论，写得真实动人，含蓄而情深。[1]

1　缪钺等：《宋诗鉴赏辞典》，上海辞书出版社1987年版，第341—343页。

於潜^①女

青裙缟袂^②於潜女，

两足如霜不穿屦^③，

觰^④沙鬌发丝穿杼^⑤，

蓬沓障前走风雨。

老潓^⑥宫妆传父祖，

至今遗民悲故主。

苕溪^⑦杨柳初飞絮，

照溪画眉渡谿^⑧去。

逢郎樵归相媚妩，

不信姬姜有齐鲁。

注释

　　①於潜：浙江古县名，在今杭州市西二百多里处。②缟袂（gǎo mèi）：白色衣服。③屦（jù）：鞋。④觰（zhā）：张开。⑤杼（zhù）：织梭。⑥潓（bì）：指汉吴王刘濞。⑦苕溪：源出浙江天目山。⑧谿（xī）：同"溪"。

A Country-woman of Yuqian

A country-woman in farm dress and skirt blue
Reveals her frost-white bare feet for she wears no shoe.
A silver hairpin passing through her tousled hair,
Like shuttle in a loom she wades in wind and rain.
Hers is the dress that ancient palace maids did wear:
People cannot forget their former master's reign.
Willow catkins begin to fly beside the brook
Which sees her pass across with her pencilled eyebrows.
The woodman comes back, they exchange an amorous look
And won't believe on earth there is a happier spouse.

赏析

　　本诗前八句描绘了於潜山村少女的天生丽质与古风浓厚的衣妆，后两句勾勒出了山村青年男子和妙龄女子无忧无虑的爱情生活。全诗清新健道，句句押韵。[1]

1　　杨萃宗：《爱情诗注析》，山西人民出版社1988年版，第587页。

行香子
过七里濑①

一叶舟轻，

双桨鸿惊。

水天清、影湛波平。

鱼翻藻鉴，

鹭点烟汀。

过沙溪急，

霜溪冷，

月溪明。

注释

　　①七里濑（lài）：在今浙江省桐庐县城南三十里。

Song of Pilgrimage
Passing the Seven-league Shallows

A leaf-like boat goes light,

At dripping oars wild geese take fright.

Under a sky serene

Clear shadows float on calm waves green.

Among the mirrored water grass fish play

And egrets dot the riverbank mist-gray.

Thus I go past

The sandy brook flowing fast,

The frosted brook cold,

The moonlit brook bright to behold.

重重似画，

曲曲如屏。

算当年、虚老严陵^①。

君臣^②一梦，

今古空名。

但远山长，

云山乱，

晓山青。

注释

　　①严陵：即严光，东汉人，曾帮助刘秀打天下。②君臣：君指刘秀，臣指严光。

Hill upon hill is a picturesque scene;

Bend after bend looks like a screen.

I recall those far-away years:

The hermit wasted his life till he grew old;

The emperor shared the same dream with his peers.

Then as now, their fame was left out in the cold.

Only the distant hills outspread

Till they're unseen,

The cloud-crowned hills look dishevelled

And dawn-lit hills so green.

赏析

本词描写了七里濑的优美景色，表现了作者对江南水乡的热爱，也流露了功名虚无、江山常在的人生哲学。[1]

1　唐圭璋等：《唐宋词鉴赏辞典（唐·五代·北宋）》，上海辞书出版社1988年版，第710—711页。

行香子
丹阳寄述古①

携手江村，

梅雪飘裙。

情何限？

处处销魂！

故人②不见，

旧曲重闻。

向望湖楼③，

孤山寺④，

涌金门⑤。

注释

①述古：杭州知州陈襄，字述古。②故人：指陈述古。③望湖楼：在杭州。④孤山寺：在杭州孤山南。⑤涌金门：杭州城之正西门。

Song of Pilgrimage
Reminiscence

We visited riverside village hand in hand,

Letting snowlike mume flowers on silk dress fall.

How can I stand

The soul-consuming fairy land!

Now severed from you for years long,

Hearing the same old song,

Can I forget the lakeside hall,

The temple on the Lonely Hill

And Golden Gate waves overfill?

寻常行处，

题诗千首，

绣罗衫、

与拂红尘。

别来相忆，

知是何人？

有湖①中月，

江边柳，

陇头云。

注释

    ①湖：指杭州西湖。

Wherever we went on whatever day,

We have written a thousand lines.

The silken sleeves would sweep the dust away.

Since we parted, who

Would often think of you?

The moon which on the lake shines,

The lakeside willow trees,

The cloud and breeze.

赏析

　　本词上片从分手写起，进而写自己回忆故人的落寞心情；下片追忆与友人同乐的情景，进而表现其思念之情。忆人与忆景融会为一，情深意切，诗意盎然，含蓄蕴藉。[1]

1　　朱靖华：《苏轼词新释辑评》，中国书店2007年版，第166—169页。

行香子
述怀

清夜无尘，

月色如银。

酒斟时、须满十分。

浮名浮利，

虚苦劳神。

叹隙中驹，

石中火，

梦中身。

虽抱文章，

开口谁亲？

且陶陶[①]、乐尽天真。

几时归去？

作个闲人。

对一张琴，

一壶酒，

一溪云。

注释

①陶陶：无忧无虑、单纯快乐的样子。

Song of Pilgrimage
Reflections

Stainless in the clear night;

The moon is silver bright.

Fill my wine cup

Till it brims up!

Why toil with pain

For wealth and fame in vain?

Time flies as a steed white

Passes a gap in flight.

Like a spark in the dark

Or a dream of moonbeam.

Though I can write,

Who thinks I'm right?

Why not enjoy

Like a mere boy?

So I would be

A man carefree.

I would be mute before my lute;

Fine before wine;

And proud as cloud.

赏析

  本词抒写了作者把酒对月之时的襟怀意绪，流露了人生苦短、知音难觅的感慨，表达了作者渴望摆脱世俗困扰的退隐、出世之意。全词语言畅达，音韵和谐，形式与内容完美地融合，并以议论表现人生感悟，很有哲理意义，为东坡词中风格旷达之作。[1]

---

1 唐圭璋等：《唐宋词鉴赏辞典（唐·五代·北宋）》，上海辞书出版社1988年版，第707—708页。

醉落魄

离京口^①作

轻云微月，

二更^②酒醒船初发。

孤城回望苍烟合。

记得歌时，

不记归时节。

巾偏扇坠藤床滑，

觉来幽梦无人说。

此生飘零何时歇？

家在西南，

常作东南别。

注释

　　①京口：今江苏镇江。②二更：指晚上九时至十一时。

Drunk with Soul Lost
Leaving the Riverside Town

The crescent moon veiled by cloud light,

I wake from wine when my boat sets sail at midnight.

Turning my head toward the mist-veiled lonely town,

I only remember the farewell song,

But not when from the wineshop I got down.

Hood wry, fan dropped, I slipped from wicker bed.

Whom can I tell the dreary dream I dread?

When from this floating life may I take rest?

My hometown in southwest,

Why do I oft in southeast bid adieu as guest?

赏析

本词描述了舟中酒醒后的心境，表达了对仕宦奔波的倦意和对家乡的思念。词之上片写酒醒，下片写梦回。这首词，语言平易质朴而又清新自然，感伤之情寓于叙事之中，将醉酒醒后思乡的心境表现得委婉动人，使人领略到作者高超的艺术表现技巧。[1]

---

1 唐圭璋等：《唐宋词鉴赏辞典（唐·五代·北宋）》，上海辞书出版社1988年版，第721—722页。

醉落魄
苏州阊门^①留别

苍颜华发，

故山归计何时决？

旧交新贵音书绝。

惟有佳人^②，

犹作殷勤别。

离亭^③欲去歌声咽，

潇潇细雨凉吹颊。

泪珠不用罗巾浥^④。

弹在罗衫，

图得见时说。

注释

　　①苏州阊（chāng）门：苏州古城之西门。②佳人：指歌女。③离亭：驿路边的亭舍。④浥（yì）：通"渑"，沾湿。

84

Drunk with Soul Lost
Farewell at the Gate of Suzhou

A pale face with hair grey,

When can I go home without care?

No word's received from my friends old or new,

Only the songstress fair

Comes to sing for me a song of adieu.

On leaving the pavilion, with sobs she sings;

The chilly breeze a drizzling rain to my cheeks brings.

Don't use your handkerchief to wipe your tears away!

Let them fall on your silken sleeves!

When we meet again, I know how it grieves.

赏析

　　本词上片写岁月蹉跎，双鬓已白，故乡归计时时未决；旧交新贵，音断书绝，佳人对我一往情深。下片写佳人因我离去而歌声凄咽，自己内心凄苦而任凉风吹颊。该词抒情之深沉婉转，令人感叹莫名。[1]

1　刘默、陈思思、黄桂月编著：《宋词鉴赏大全集 上》，中国华侨出版社2012年版，第175页。

南乡子
送述古

回首乱山横，

不见居人只见城。

谁似临平山①上塔，

亭亭，

迎客西来送客行。

归路晚风清，

一枕初寒梦不成。

今夜残灯斜照处，

荧荧②，

秋雨晴时泪不晴。

注释

　　①临平山：在杭州东北。②荧荧：指泪光。

Song of Southern Country
Farewell to a Friend

Turning my head, I find rugged mountains bar the sky,

I can no longer see you in the town.

Who can be like the hilltop tower looking down,

So high?

It welcomed you from the west and bids you goodbye.

I come back at dusk in a gentle breeze.

On chilly pillow how can I dream with ease?

Where will the flickering lamp shed its lonely light tonight?

When autumn rain no longer falls drop by drop,

Oh, will tears stop?

赏析

　　这是一首送别之作，表达了词人情真意切的送别之情。词的上片回叙分手后回望离别之地临平镇和临平山，抒写了对往事无限美好的回忆和对友人的依恋之情；下片则述归来怀念之情。友人既已远逝，回家的路上晚风凄清。全词写得情真意切，大气磅礴。[1]

1　唐圭璋等：《唐宋词鉴赏辞典（唐·五代·北宋）》，上海辞书出版社1988年版，第656页。

南乡子
梅花词和杨元素①

寒雀满疏篱,

争抱寒柯②看玉蕤③。

忽见客来花下坐,

惊飞。

蹴散芳英落酒卮④。

痛饮又能诗,

坐客无毡醉不知。

花尽酒阑春到也,

离离⑤。

一点微霜已著枝。

注释

　　①杨元素:即杨绘,字元素。②柯:树枝。③蕤(ruí):花茂盛的样子。④酒卮(zhī):酒杯。⑤离离:繁盛的样子。

Song of Southern Country
Mume Blossoms for Yang Yuansu

On the fence perch birds feeling cold,

To view the blooms of jade they dispute for branch old.

Seeing a guest sit under flowers, they fly up

And scatter petals over his wine cup.

Writing verses and drinking wine,

The guest knows not he's not sitting on felt fine.

Wine cup dried up, spring comes with fallen flower.

Leave here! The branch has felt a little sour.

赏析

　　本词上片实写己方观梅，梅之清幽、高寒，从寒雀集枝、争看花朵传出。下片虚写对方观梅，梅之高格、雅韵，从雅士流连、诗酒风流传出。全词不施刻画，离形取神，虚实结合。读来饶有余味。[1]

1　刘默、陈思思、黄桂月编著：《宋词鉴赏大全集 上》，中国华侨出版社2012年版，第146页。

南乡子

集句

怅望送春杯，（杜牧）

渐老逢春能几回？（杜甫）

花满楚城愁远别，（许浑）

伤怀，

何况清丝急管催？（刘禹锡）

吟断望乡台，（李商隐）

万里归心独上来。（许浑）

景物登临闲始见，（杜牧）

徘徊，

一寸相思一寸灰。（李商隐）

注释

①送春杯：指送春酒。②清丝：指丝弦乐器。

90

Song of Southern Country

Wine cup in hand, I see spring off in vain. (Du Mu)

How many times can I, oldened, see spring again? (Du Fu)

The town in bloom, I'm grieved to be far, far away. (Xu Hun)

Can I be gay?

The pipes and strings do hasten spring not to delay. (Liu Yuxi)

I croon and gaze from Homesick Terrace high; (Li Shangyin)

Coming for miles and miles, alone I mount and sigh. (Xu Hun)

Things can be best enjoyed in a leisurely way; (Du Mu)

For long I stay,

And inch by inch my heart burns into ashes grey. (Li Shangyin)

赏析

　　这首词是苏轼贬谪黄州的词作，既有他为人熟知的豁达开朗、处之泰然的一面，亦有痛苦、挣扎的灰暗一面。全词取唐人诗句不仅均符合词人当下的境遇、身世、心态，而且信手拈来，仿若己出，经过他贯注心血的再创造获得了新的生命力。[1]

1　谢真元主编：《一生必读宋词三百首鉴赏》，中国对外翻译出版公司2007年版，第531页。

江城子
湖上与张先同赋

凤凰山①下雨初晴。

水风清。

晚霞明。

一朵芙蕖②、开过尚盈盈。

何处飞来双白鹭？

如有意，

慕娉婷。

忽闻江上弄哀筝。

苦含情。

遣谁听？

烟敛云收、依约是湘灵③。

欲待曲终寻问取，

人不见，

数峰青。

注释

①凤凰山：在杭州西湖之南。②芙蕖（qú）：即荷花。③湘灵：古代传说中的湘水之神。

Riverside Town
On the Lake

It turns fine after rain below the Phoenix Hill,

Waves and wind light,

Rainbow clouds bright.

A lotus flower past full bloom beams with smile still.

Where comes in flight

A pair of egrets white

As if inclined to care

For maidens fair.

Suddenly on the stream music comes to the ear.

Who would not hear

Such feeling drear?

Away clouds and mist clear;

The Spirit of River Xiang seems to appear.

When music ends, I would inquire for the lutist dear.

She seems to disappear,

Only leaving peaks clear.

赏析

　　本词上片写湖上景，下片写闻弹筝。全词采用比喻和衬托的手法，写弹筝而不见弹筝人，而以闻筝所见和想象来营造其美妙的意境。[1]

1　　唐圭璋等：《唐宋词鉴赏辞典（唐·五代·北宋）》，上海辞书出版社1988年版，第686—687页。

昭君怨
送别

谁作桓伊^①三弄，
惊破绿窗^②幽梦？
新月与愁烟，
满江天。

欲去又还不去，
明日落花飞絮。
飞絮送行舟，
水东流。

注释

　　①桓伊：东晋时音乐家，善筝笛。②绿窗：罩有碧纱的窗子，诗词中多指女子居室。

君不見詩人借車無可載，留得一錢何足賴。
晨穿老屋漏絲絲，夜卧空堂鼠嚙嚙。
作詩解嘲愁肝腎，...

宋 蘇軾 書次韻秦太虛見戲耳聾詩 台北故宮博物院藏

宋 苏轼 书次韵三舍人省上诗 台北故宫博物院藏

Lament of a Fair Lady

Who's playing on the flute a gloomy tune:
Breaking the green window's dreary dream?
The dreary mist veils the new moon.
Outspread in the sky over the stream.

You linger still though you must go.
Afraid flowers and willow down will fall tomorrow.
How could the stream not eastward flow?
Let willow down follow your boat laden with sorrow!

赏析

　　本词上阕写送别情景，渲染出送别时的感伤氛围；下阕运用叠句造境传情，想象来日分别的情景。全词景色凄迷，离思缠绵。在写法上虚实结合，构思新颖，不落俗套，渲染出一种强烈的情感氛围，具有极强的艺术感染力。[1]

1　唐圭璋等：《唐宋词鉴赏辞典（唐·五代·北宋）》，上海辞书出版社1988年版，第668—670页。

瑞鹧鸪

观潮

碧山影里小红旗，

侬是江南踏浪儿^①。

拍手欲嘲山简^②醉，

齐声争唱浪婆^③词。

西兴渡口帆初落，

渔浦山头日未欹^④。

侬欲送潮歌底^⑤曲，

樽前还唱使君诗。

注释

　　①踏浪儿：参加水戏的选手。②山简：字季伦，晋时人，好酒。
③浪婆：波浪之神。④欹（qī）：倾斜。⑤底：什么。

Auspicious Partridge
Watching the Tidal Bore

In the shade of blue hills small red flags undulate,

You are sons of the Southerners treading waves green.

Clapping your hands, you laugh at the drunk magistrate;

In unison, you vie to sing "Goddess Marine".

Sails have just lowered down in the Ferry Xixing;

Atop Yupu hills the sun begins to decline.

If you want to see the tide fall, what will you sing?

It's your magistrate's song before a cup of wine.

赏析

　　本词上片写弄潮儿在万顷波中自由、活泼的形象。下片写钱塘江退潮，弄潮儿唱起"使君诗"作为送潮曲。此词语言平实，亲切有味，用笔精炼含蓄。[1]

1　陈迩冬：《苏东坡诗词选》，人民文学出版社1982年版，第94页。

虞美人
有美堂赠述古

湖山信是东南美，

一望弥千里。

使君能得几回来？

便使樽前醉倒、更徘徊。

沙河塘①里灯初上，

水调谁家唱？

夜阑风静欲归时，

惟有一江明月、碧琉璃。

注释

　①沙河塘：在杭州城东南。

The Beautiful Lady Yu
Written for Chen Xiang at the Scenic Hall

How fair the lakes and hills of the Southeast land are,
With plains extending wide and far!
How oft, wine-cup in hand, have you been here
That you can make us linger though drunk we appear?

By Sandy River Pond the new-lit lamps are bright.
Who is singing "the water melody" at night?
When I come back, the wind goes down, the bright moon paves
With emerald glass the river waves.

赏析

　　本词上片写揽景兴怀，通过对有美堂景色的描写，表达了词人对友人的依依不舍之情。下片描写华灯初上时杭州的繁华景象，将词人内心的不舍与惜别之情表达得淋漓尽致。全词以美的意象带来了极高的艺术享受，同时也将词人与友人的感情至深展现得一览无余。[1]

1　林力、肖剑主编：《宋词鉴赏大典（上、中、下卷）》，长征出版社1999年版，第355—356页。

少年游
润州作，代人寄远

去年相送，

余杭门①外，

飞雪似杨花。

今年春尽，

杨花似雪，

犹不见还家。

对酒卷帘邀明月，

风露透窗纱。

恰似姮娥②怜双燕，

分明照、画梁斜。

注释

①余杭门：北宋时杭州的北门之一。②姮娥：即嫦娥。

Wandering Youth
Written for a Friend

Last year we bade adieu
Outside the town;
Snow flew like willow down.
This year spring dies,
Like snow willow down flies,
But I can't come back to see you.

The screen uprolled, to wine I invite the moon bright;
Through the window the breeze brings in dew.
The Moon Goddess seems to care
For the swallows in pair.
She sheds her light
Into their dream on painted beam.

赏析

  词上片写夫妻别离时间之久，诉说亲人不当别而别、当归而未归；下片转写夜晚，着意刻画妻子对月思人的孤寂与惆怅。词用飞雪似杨花和杨花似雪这两个比喻贯穿上片，结构精致，文思巧妙，营造出一种幽深、缠绵的意境，感人肺腑。[1]

---

1 李静等：《唐诗宋词鉴赏大全集》，华文出版社2009年版，第255页。

密州：老夫聊发少年狂

沁园春
赴密州，早行，马上寄子由

孤馆灯青，

野店鸡号，

旅枕梦残。

渐月华收练，

晨霜耿耿①；

云山摛锦②，

朝露溥溥③。

世路无穷，

劳生有限，

似此区区长鲜欢。

微吟罢，

凭征鞍无语，

往事千端。

注释

①耿耿：明亮的样子。②摛（chī）锦：似锦缎展开。③溥溥（tuán）：露盛多的样子。

106

Spring in a Pleasure Garden
Written to Ziyou on My Way to Mizhou

The lamp burns with green flames in an inn's lonely hall,

The wayfarer's dream is broken by the cock's call.

Slowly the blooming moon rolls up her silk dress white,

The frost begins to shimmer in the soft daylight;

The cloud-crowned hills outspread their brocade

And morning dews glitter like pearls displayed.

As the way of the world is long,

But our toilsome life short,

So, for a man like me, joyless is oft my sort.

After humming this song,

Silent, on my saddle I lean,

Brooding over the past scene after scene.

当时共客长安，

似二陆①初来俱少年。

有笔头千字，

胸中万卷；

致君②尧舜，

此事何难！

用舍由时，

行藏在我，

袖手何妨闲处看。

身长健，

但优游卒岁，

且斗樽前。

注释

①二陆：指西晋文学家陆机、陆云兄弟。②致君：辅佐国君，使其成为圣明之主。

Together then to the capital we came,

Like the two Brothers Lu of literary fame.

A fluent pen combined

With a widely-read mind,

Why could we not have helped the Crown

To attain great renown?

As times require,

I advance or retire,

With folded arms I may stand by.

If we keep fit,

We may enjoy life before we lose it.

So drink the wine-cup dry!

赏析

　　本词由景入情，由今入昔，直抒胸臆，表达了作者人生遭遇的不幸和壮志难酬的苦闷。上片写早行，感叹世路无穷，日日如此奔波，劳生有限。下片回忆嘉祐初汴京往事，写报国抱负未能得到充分施展的感慨。[1]

1　唐圭璋等：《唐宋词鉴赏辞典（唐·五代·北宋）》，上海辞书出版社1988年版，第623—625页。

江城子
密州出猎

老夫聊发少年狂，
左牵黄，
右擎苍。
锦帽貂裘，
千骑卷平岗。
为报倾城随太守，
亲射虎，
看孙郎。

酒酣胸胆尚开张。
鬓微霜，
又何妨！
持节云中，
何日遣冯唐？
会挽雕弓如满月，
西北望，
射天狼。

Riverside Town
Hunting at Mizhou

Rejuvenated, my fiery zeal I display:
Left hand leashing a yellow hound,
On the right wrist a falcon gray.
A thousand silk-capped and sable-coated horsemen sweep
Across the rising ground
And hillocks steep.
Townspeople come out of the city gate
To watch the tiger-hunting magistrate.

Heart gladdened with strong wine, who cares
For a few frosted hairs?
When will the imperial court send
Me as envoy with flags and banners? Then I'll bend
My bow like a full moon, and aiming northwest, I
Will shoot down the Wolf from the sky.

赏析

　　本词创作于作者知密州任上，表达了强国抗敌的政治主张，抒写了渴望报效朝廷的慷慨意气和壮志豪情。全词"狂"态毕露，虽不乏慷慨激愤之情，但气象恢弘，一反词作柔弱的格调，充满阳刚之美。[1]

1　吴熊和：《唐宋词汇评·两宋卷（一）》，浙江教育出版社2004年版，第473—474页。

蝶恋花
密州上元

灯火钱塘三五①夜，

明月如霜，

照见人如画。

帐底吹笙香吐麝，

更无一点尘随马。

寂寞山城②人老也，

击鼓吹箫，

却入农桑社。

火冷灯稀霜露下，

昏昏雪意云垂野。

注释

①三五夜：即每月十五日夜，此处指元宵节。②山城：指密州。

Butterfly in Love with Flower
Lantern Festival at Mizhou

On Lantern Festival by riverside at night,

The moon frost-white

Shone on the beauties fair and bright.

Fragrance exhaled and music played under the tent,

The running horses raised no dust on the pavement.

Now I am old in lonely hillside town,

Drumbeats and flute songs up and down

Are drowned in prayers amid mulberries and lost.

The lantern fires put out, dew falls with frost.

Over the fields dark clouds hangs low:

It threatens snow.

赏析

　　本词上阕描写杭州元宵景致，下阕描写密州上元，前后对比，写出了密州上元的寂寞冷清，流露出作者对杭州的思念和初来密州时的寂寞心情。全词内容、笔墨不囿于成规，自抒胸臆，意之所到，笔亦随之，不求工而自工。[1]

1　唐圭璋等 :《唐宋词鉴赏辞典（唐・五代・北宋）》，上海辞书出版社1988年版，第699—701页。

水调歌头
明月几时有

丙辰中秋，欢饮达旦，大醉，作此篇，兼怀子由。

明月几时有？
把酒问青天。
不知天上宫阙，
今夕是何年？
我欲乘风归去，
又恐琼楼玉宇，
高处不胜寒。
起舞弄清影，
何似在人间？

Prelude to Water Melody
Sent to Ziyou on Mid-autumn Festival

On the mid-autumn festival, I drank happily till dawn and wrote this in my cups while thinking of Ziyou.

When did the bright moon first appear?
Wine-cup in hand, I ask the blue sky.
I do not know what time of year
It would be tonight in the palace on high.
Riding the wind, there I would fly,
But I'm afraid the crystalline palace would be
Too high and too cold for me.
I rise and dance, with my shadow I play.
On high as on earth, would it be as gay?

转朱阁，

低绮户，

照无眠。

不应有恨，

何事长向别时圆？

人有悲欢离合，

月有阴晴圆缺，

此事古难全。

但愿人长久，

千里共婵娟。

The moon goes round the mansions red

With gauze windows to shed

Her light upon the sleepless bed.

Against man she should not have any spite.

Why then when people part is she oft full and bright?

Men have sorrow and joy, they part and meet again;

The moon may be bright or dim, she may wax or wane.

There has been nothing perfect since olden days.

So let us wish that man live as long as he can!

Though miles apart, we'll share the beauty she displays.

赏析

　　熙宁九年中秋，词人在与胞弟分别七年后，面对一轮明月，心潮起伏，于是乘酒兴正酣，挥笔写下了这首名篇。全词立意高远，构思新颖，意境清新如画，极富哲理与人情，具有很高的审美价值。此词全篇皆是佳句，集中体现出苏词清雄旷达的风格。[1]

1　唐圭璋等：《唐宋词鉴赏辞典（唐·五代·北宋）》，上海辞书出版社1988年版，第611—614页。

江城子
乙卯正月二十日夜记梦

十年生死两茫茫，

不思量，

自难忘。

千里孤坟，

无处话凄凉。

纵使相逢应不识：

尘满面，

鬓如霜。

夜来幽梦忽还乡。

小轩窗，

正梳妆。

相顾无言，

惟有泪千行。

料得年年肠断处：

明月夜，

短松冈。

Riverside Town

Dreaming of My Deceased Wife on the Night of the 20th Day of the 1st Month ①

For ten long years the living of the dead knows nought.

Should the dead be forgot

And to mind never brought?

Her lonely grave is a thousand miles away.

To whom can I my grief convey?

Revived e'en if she be, could she still know me?

My face is worn with care

And frosted is my hair.

Last night I dreamed of coming to my native place:

She's making up her face

At the window with grace.

We gazed at each other hushed,

But tears from our eyes gushed.

When I am woken, I fancy her heart-broken

On the mound clad with pines,

Where only the moon shines.

赏析

　　苏轼为悼念原配妻子王弗而创作的一首悼亡词。上阕记实，下阕记梦，虚实结合，衬托出对亡妻的思念，加深全词的悲伤基调。[1]

1　唐圭璋等：《唐宋词鉴赏辞典（唐·五代·北宋）》，上海辞书出版社1988年版，第693—694页。

更漏子
送孙巨源①

水涵空②，

山照市，

西汉二疏③乡里。

新白发，

旧黄金，

故人恩义深。

海东头，

山尽处，

自古客槎④来去。

槎有信，

赴秋期，

使君⑤行不归。

注释

①孙巨源：孙洙，字巨源，苏轼友人。②涵空：指水映天空。③西汉二疏：即疏广、疏受，两人为叔侄。④槎（chá）：木筏。⑤使君：此处是指孙巨源。

Song of Water Clock
Seeing Sun Juyuan off

The water joins the sky,

The town girt with hills high,

This is a land of talents as of yore.

Your hair has turned white,

Of gold you make light,

You value friendship more.

East of the sea,

Where end the hills you see,

Boats come and go since days of old.

They have a date;

For you I'll wait.

Will you come back with autumn cold?

赏析

　　此词为送别词，词的上片用西汉二疏（疏广、疏受）故事赞颂孙洙，下片以乘槎故事叙说别情。在词中，作者将仕途中的无穷忧患情思与自己的身世感慨融合一起，表达了极为复杂的心绪。[1]

1　唐圭璋等：《唐宋词鉴赏辞典（唐·五代·北宋）》，上海辞书出版社1988年版，第719页。

永遇乐
寄孙巨源

长忆别时，

景疏楼①上，

明月如水。

美酒清歌，

留连不住，

月随人千里。

别来三度，

孤光又满，

冷落共谁同醉？

卷珠帘、凄然顾影，

共伊到明无寐。

注释

①景疏楼：在海州东北。

Joy of Eternal Union
For Sun Juyuan

I long remember when we bade goodbye

On Northeast Tower high,

The silvery moonlight looked like water bright.

But songs and wine, however fine,

Could not keep you from going away.

Only the moon followed you for miles on your way.

Since we parted, I've seen the moon wax and wane.

But who would drink with lonely me again?

Uprolling the screen,

Only my shadow's seen,

I stay awake until daybreak.

今朝有客，

来从滩①上，

能道使君深意。

凭仗清淮，

分明到海，

中有相思泪。

而今何在？

西垣②清禁③，

夜永露华侵被。

此时看、回廊晓月，

也应暗记。

注释

①滩（suī）：水名，自河南经安徽，流入江苏。②西垣：中书省。③
清禁：宫中。

Today your friend comes from the river's end,

And brings to me your memory.

You ask the river clear

To bring nostalgic tear

As far as the east sea.

I do not know now where are you.

In palace hall by western wall,

Is your coverlet in deep night wet with dew?

When you see in the corridor the moving moonrays,

Could you forget the bygone days?

赏析

　　本词上片由设想巨源当初离别海州时写起，以月为抒情线索展开回忆，表达了词人对友人的怀念之情。下片通过对周围景象的描写，更加渲染了词人内心的思念以及回忆。全词通过借景抒情的表现手法，将词人内心对友人的思念之情表达得淋漓尽致。[1]

1　唐圭璋等：《唐宋词鉴赏辞典（唐·五代·北宋）》，上海辞书出版社1988年版，第703—704页。

江城子
孤山竹阁送述古

翠蛾羞黛怯人看，

掩霜纨[1]，

泪偷弹。

且尽一尊，

收泪唱《阳关》。

漫道帝城天样远，

天易见，

见君难。

画堂新构近孤山，

曲栏干，

为谁安？

飞絮落花，

春色属[2]明年。

欲棹[3]小舟寻旧事，

无处问，

水连天。

注释

　　①霜纨（wán）：指白纨扇。②属：同"嘱"，嘱托。③棹（zhào）：船桨。

Riverside Town

Farewell to Governor Chen at Bamboo Pavilion on Lonely Hill

Her eyebrows penciled dark, she feels shy to be seen.

Hidden behind a silken fan so green,

Stealthily she sheds tear on tear.

Let me drink farewell to you and hear

Her sing, with tears wiped away, her song of adieu.

Do not say the imperial town is as far as the sky.

It is easier to see the sun high

Than to meet you.

The newly built painted hall to Lonely Hill is near.

For whom is made

The winding balustrade?

Falling flowers and willow down fly;

Spring belongs to next year.

I try to row a boat to find the things gone by.

O whom can I ask? In my eye

I only see water one with the sky.

赏析

　　这首词上阕描述歌妓在饯别时的情景，下阕模写歌妓的相思之情。词中传神地描摹歌妓的口气，代她向即将由杭州调知南都的僚友陈述古表示惜别之意。[1]

1　朱靖华：《苏轼词新释辑评》，中国书店2007年版，第217—220页。

宋 苏轼 致主簿曹君尺牍 台北故宫博物院藏

辭歸去來兮

余家貧耕植不足以自給幼稚盈
室缾無儲粟生生所資未見其術
親故多勸余為長吏脫然有懷求
之靡途會有四方之事諸侯以惠
愛為德家叔以余貧苦遂見用於
小邑於時風波未靜心憚遠役彭
澤去家百里公田之利足以為酒
故便求之及少日眷然有歸歟之情何則

宋 苏轼 书归去来兮辞卷（局部） 台北故宫博物院藏

徐州：问言豆叶几时黄

阳关曲
中秋作

暮云收尽溢清寒，
银汉无声转玉盘。
此生此夜不长好，
明月明年何处看？

Song of the Sunny Pass
The Mid-autumn Moon

Evening clouds withdrawn, pure cold air floods the sky;

The River of Stars mute, a jade plate turns on high.

How oft can we enjoy a fine mid-autumn night?

Where shall we view next year a silver moon so bright?

赏析

　　本词记述的是作者与其胞弟苏辙久别重逢，共赏中秋月的赏心乐事，同时也抒发了聚后不久又得分手的哀伤与感慨。[1]

1　唐圭璋等：《唐宋词鉴赏辞典（唐·五代·北宋）》，上海辞书出版社1988年版，第724—725页。

浣溪沙
徐门石潭谢雨，道上作五首

一

照日深红暖见鱼，

连村绿暗晚藏乌。

黄童白叟聚睢盱[1]。

麋鹿逢人虽未惯，

猿猱[2]闻鼓不须呼。

归来说与采桑姑。

二

旋抹红妆看使君，

三三五五棘篱门。

相排踏破茜罗裙。

老幼扶携收麦社，

乌鸢翔舞赛神村。

道逢醉叟卧黄昏。

注释

　　①睢（suī）盱（xū）：喜悦高兴的样子。②猿猱（náo）：猿类的一种。

Silk-washing Stream
Thanks for Rain at Stony Pool

I

In warm sunlight the Pool turns red where fish can be seen,
And trees can shelter crows at dusk with shades dark green.
With eyes wide open, old and young come out to see me.

Like deer the kids are not accustomed strangers to meet;
Like monkeys they appear unbidden as drums beat.
Back, they tell sisters picking leaves of mulberry.

II

Maidens make up in haste to see the magistrate;
By threes and fives they come out at their hedgerow gate.
They push and squeeze and trample each other's skirt red.

Villagers old and young to celebration are led;
With crows and kites they dance thanksgiving in array.
At dusk I see an old man lie drunk on my way.

三

麻叶层层檾①叶光，

谁家煮茧一村香？

隔篱娇语络丝娘。

垂白杖藜抬醉眼，

捋②青③捣㦬④软饥肠。

问言豆叶几时黄？

四

簌簌衣巾落枣花，

村南村北响缫车⑤。

牛衣古柳卖黄瓜。

酒困路长惟欲睡，

日高人渴漫思茶。

敲门试问野人家。

注释

　　①檾（qǐng）：同"苘"，俗称青麻。②捋（luō）：用手握住条状物向一端滑动。③青：指新麦。④㦬（chǎo）：用麦子制成的干粮。⑤缫（sāo）车：纺车。

III

The leaves of jute and hemp are thick and lush in this land;
The scent of boiling cocoons in the village spreads.
Across the fence young maidens prate while reeling threads.

An old man raises dim-sighted eyes, cane in hand;
He picks new wheat so that his hunger he may ease.
I wonder when will yellow the leaves of green peas.

IV

Date flowers fall in showers on my hooded head;
At both ends of the village wheels are spinning thread;
A straw-cloaked man sells cucumbers 'neath a willow tree.

Wine-drowsy when the road is long, I yearn for bed;
Throat parched when the sun is high, I long for tea.
I knock at farmer's door to see to what he'll treat me.

五

软草平莎①过雨新，

轻沙走马路无尘。

何时收拾耦耕②身？

日暖桑麻光似泼，

风来蒿艾气如薰。

使君元③是此中人。

注释

①莎（suō）：莎草。②耦（ǒu）耕：泛指耕作。③元：通"原"。

V

After rain the paddy fields look fresh as soft grass;

No dust is raised on sandy roads where horses pass.

When can I come to till the ground with household mine?

Hemp and mulberry glint as if steeped in sunshine;

Mugwort and moxa spread a sweet scent in the breeze.

I remember I was companion of all these.

赏析

　　本词是苏轼任徐州太守时求雨后到石潭谢雨途中所作。这五首词将农村题材带入北宋词坛，给词坛带来了朴素清新的乡土气息，为农村词的发展开创了良好的文风，在题材上完全突破了"词为艳科"的藩篱，具有开拓性意义。[1]

1　夏承焘等：《苏轼诗文鉴赏辞典》，上海辞书出版社2012年版，第429—436页。

浣溪沙

山色横侵①蘸②晕霞③，
湘川④风静吐寒花⑤。
远林屋散尚啼鸦。

梦到故园多少路？
酒醒南望隔天涯。
月明千里照平沙。

注释

①横侵：纵横扩展。②蘸（zhàn）：以液体沾染他物。③晕霞：这里指晚霞。④湘川：此处指湖北古荆州地区。⑤寒花：多指菊花。

Silk-washing Stream

The sky is barred with mountains steeped in flushing cloud;
The windless Southern Stream exhales cold blossoms proud;
Cottages in far-off woods with crying crows are still loud.

How far away in dreams, oh! is my native land!
Awake from wine, I find sky-scraping mountains stand;
For miles and miles the moon shines on the plain of sand.

赏析

本词上片淋漓尽致地描写了深秋的景色，下片是作者对梦到故乡的具体描写。全词即景抒情，如行云流水，是写实之作。[1]

1　王筱云：《宋词三百首》，大连出版社1999年版，第62页。

浣溪沙

风压轻云贴水飞，
乍晴池馆燕争泥。
沈郎多病不胜衣。

沙上不闻鸿雁信，
竹间时听鹧鸪啼。
此情惟有落花知。

Silk-washing Stream

Pressed by the breeze, over water the light clouds fly;
In pecking clods by poolside tower swallows vie.
I feel too weak to wear my gown, ill for so long.

I have not heard the message-bearing wild geese's song;
Partridges among bamboos seem to call me go home;
Only fallen blooms know the heart of those who roam.

赏析

  全词仅上片开头两句写景，第三句抒情，用的是先实后虚的手法。下片则虚实结合，情中见景。在苏轼笔下，不仅"一切景语皆情语也"（王国维《人间词话》），而且于情语中也往往见景物。这是一种很高妙的手法。[1]

---

1 唐圭璋等：《唐宋词鉴赏辞典（唐·五代·北宋）》，上海辞书出版社1988年版，第742页。

浣溪沙
咏橘

菊暗荷枯一夜霜，
新苞绿叶照林光。
竹篱茅舍出青黄。

香雾噀人惊半破，
清泉流齿怯初尝。
吴姬三日手犹香。

Silk-washing Stream
The Tangerine

After one night of frost
Chrysanthemums are darkened and lotus flowers lost.
The wood is brightened by leaves green and buds new,
The thatched cot and fence would grow yellow and blue.

Her mouth half open, she smells the fragrance sweet;
She's timid to drink the fountain her teeth meet.
Her hand still fragrant stays for three long days.

赏析

  本词上片写橘树耐寒的品性和生长的盛景，下片写出品尝新橘的情状和橘果的清香，结句以"三日手犹香"来突出橘果之香。全词描绘细致，形神兼备，饱有余味。作者借咏橘之题材以抒发自己清新高洁之性情。[1]

---

1 唐圭璋等：《唐宋词鉴赏辞典（唐·五代·北宋）》，上海辞书出版社1988年版，第733—734页。

永遇乐

彭城夜宿燕子楼，梦盼盼，因作此词。

明月如霜，

好风如水，

清景无限。

曲港跳鱼，

圆荷泻露，

寂寞无人见。

紞如①三鼓，

铿然②一叶，

黯黯梦云惊断。

夜茫茫，

重寻无处，

觉来小园行遍。

注释

①紞（dǎn）如：击鼓声。②铿（kēng）然：清越的音响。

146

Joy of Eternal Union
The Pavilion of Swallows

I lodged at the Pavilion of Swallows in Pengcheng, dreamed of the fair lady
Panpan, and wrote the following poem.

The bright moonlight is like frost white,
The gentle breeze like water clean:
Far and wide extends the night scene.
In the haven fish leap
And dew-drops roll down lotus leaves
In solitude no man perceives.
Drums beat thrice in the night so deep,
A leaf falls with a tinkling sound so loud
That gloomy, I awake from my dream of the Cloud.
Under the boundless pall of night,
Nowhere again can she be found
Though in the small garden I have walked around.

天涯倦客，

山中归路，

望断故园心眼①。

燕子楼空，

佳人何在？

空锁楼中燕。

古今如梦，

何曾梦觉？

但有旧欢新怨。

异时对、黄楼②夜景，

为余浩叹！

注释

①心眼：心愿。②黄楼：徐州东门上的大楼，苏轼任徐州知州时建造。

A tired wayfarer far from home.

In the mountains may roam,

His native land from view is blocked.

The Pavilion of Swallows is empty.

Where is the lady so fair?

In the Pavilion only swallows' nest is locked.

Both the past and the present are like dreams,

From which we have ne'er been awake, it seems.

We have but joys and sorrows old and new.

Some other day others will come to view

The Yellow Tower's night scenery,

Then they would sigh for me!

赏析

　　本词上片寻梦，以倒叙笔法写惊梦游园；下片感梦，作者登高远眺，直抒感慨。全词将景、情、理熔于一炉，传达了一种携带某种禅意玄思的人生空幻、淡漠感，隐藏着某种要求彻底解脱的出世意念，意境清旷，余味悠然。[1]

―――――――――

1　唐圭璋等：《唐宋词鉴赏辞典（唐·五代·北宋）》，上海辞书出版社1988年版，第704—706页。

南歌子

湖州作

山雨潇潇过，

溪桥浏浏^①清。

小园幽榭枕苹汀。

门外月华如水、

彩舟横。

苕^②岸霜花尽，

江湖雪阵平。

两山遥指海门青。

回首水云何处、

觅孤城？

注释

①浏浏：水流清澈的样子。②苕（tiáo）：芦苇的花。

A Southern Song
Written at Lakeside County

Shower on shower passes o'er the hills,

Clear, clear water flows 'neath bridges in the rills.

A garden pillows its bower amid the weed.

Outdoors in liquid moonlight lies afloat

A painted boat.

Frost cleared away on rivershore,

By waterside snow lingering no more.

Afar stands the blue gate to which two mountains lead.

Looking back, I find cloud and water up and down.

Where is the lonely town?

赏析

　　本词前后阕末句下七字，盖现成唐诗句，只是句头加两字也，岂可割裂耶。全词描写闺情，细致入微，描摹如画，是婉约词中的佳作。[1]

1　唐圭璋等：《唐宋词鉴赏辞典（唐·五代·北宋）》，上海辞书出版社1988年版，第662—663页。

续丽人行并引

李仲谋家有周昉画背面欠伸内人，极精，戏作此诗。

深宫无人春日长，
沉香亭北百花香。
美人睡起薄梳洗，
燕舞莺啼空断肠。
画工欲画无穷意，
背立东风初破睡①。
若教回首却嫣然，
阳城下蔡俱风靡。
杜陵饥客②眼长寒，
蹇驴破帽随金鞍。

注释

①初破睡：刚刚睡起。②杜陵饥客：指杜甫。

Song of a Fair Lady

I saw an excellent picture drawn by Zhou Fan of a yawning lady singer viewed from the back, and I wrote this poem in joke as a companion poem of Du Fu's.

In the lonely deep palace the spring days were long.
North of the Fragrance Pavilion flowers smelt sweet.
The lightly-dressed fair lady got up at the song
Of orioles, her heart broke to see swallows fleet.
The painter tried to retain her infinite charm
And paint'd her back when, awake, she stood in the east wind.
If she turned her head with a smile, she would disarm
A besieging army, however disciplined.
The hungry poet Du Fu with a longing eye,
In shabby hat and on lame ass, followed a horse.

隔花临水时一见，
只许腰肢背后看。
心醉归来茅屋底，
方信人间有西子。
君不见孟光举案与眉齐，
何曾背面伤春啼！

Sometime across the flowery stream he passed by,

He saw but from the back her slender waist and torse.

Fascinated, he came back to his thatched cot,

And then believed on earth there was a lady fair.

Don't you know man and wife were happy with their lot?

Why should she turn her back and weep with a love-sick air?

赏析

《丽人行》本为杜甫所作，写杨国忠兄妹等人郊游曲江情景。苏轼作"续"诗，语多幽默调侃，所以称为"戏作"。

除夜大雪，留潍州，元日早晴，遂行，中途雪复作

除夜雪相留，

元日晴相送。

东风吹宿酒，

瘦马兀①残梦。

葱昽晓光开，

旋转馀②花弄。

下马成野酌，

佳哉谁与共！

须臾晚云合，

乱洒无缺空。

鹅毛垂马鬃，

自怪骑白凤。

三年东方旱，

逃户连敧栋③；

老农释耒④叹，

泪入饥肠痛。

注释

①兀：昏沉的样子。②馀：通"余"。③敧栋：倾斜破败的房屋。④耒：古代农具，形状像木叉。

Snow on New Year's Day

I was detained by a heavy snow at Weizhou on New Year's Eve, but on the morning of the first day it cleared and I resumed my journey. Along the way, it started to snow again.

Detained by snow on New Year's Eve,
On fine New Year's Day I take leave.
The east wind sobers me, though drunk deep,
My lean horse jerks me out of sleep,
Faintly and softly the day breaks,
From branches whirl down last snowflakes.
I dismount afield to take wine,
But none partake my drink divine.
Suddenly dark clouds gather quick,
And heavy snow falls fast and thick.
Like goose feathers it hangs down my horse's mane.
Am I on a phoenix without stain?
For three years the east saw drought rage
And the poor desert their village.
A peasant lays aside his plow and sighs,
His starving guts ache with tears from his eyes.

春雪虽云晚，
春麦犹可种。
敢怨行役劳，
助尔歌饭瓮。

Although spring snow comes rather late,

Wheat can be sown at any rate.

Of hard journey can I complain?

———I write this to allay your pain.

赏析

　　本诗作于熙宁十年元日，苏轼奉诏离密州移知河中府赴任途中。潍州即今山东潍坊市，在密州西北约七十公里。年节时分，大雪纷飞，东坡在旅途中。他没有抱怨行役的艰辛，倒更多希望瑞雪预兆着丰年，使连年遭受蝗旱灾害的农民得到安乐。

李思训①画长江绝岛图

山苍苍，

水茫茫，

大孤②小孤③江中央。

崖崩路绝猿鸟去，

惟有乔木搀天长。

客舟何处来？

棹歌④中流声抑扬。

沙平风软望不到，

孤山久与船低昂。

峨峨两烟鬟，

晓镜开新妆。

舟中贾客莫漫狂，

小姑⑤前年嫁彭郎⑥。

注释

①李思训：唐代山水画家。②大孤：大孤山，在今江西九江鄱阳湖中。③小孤：小孤山，在今江西彭泽县古城西北的长江中。④棹歌：划船人的歌声。⑤小姑：指小孤山。⑥彭郎：即彭浪矶，在小孤山对面。

Two Lonely Isles in the Yangzi River
—Written on a Picture
Drawn by Li Sixun

Below the mountains green

Water runs till unseen;

In the midst of the stream two lonely isles stand high.

Fallen crags bar the way;

Birds and apes cannot stay;

Only the giant trees tower into the sky.

From where comes a sail white?

In mid-stream rises oarsmen's undulating song.

Sand bar is flat, the wind is weak, no boat in sight,

The Lonely Isles sink and swim with the sail for long,

Like mist-veiled tresses of a pretty lass

Using the river as her looking glass.

O merchant in the boat, don't go mad for the fair!

The Lonely Isle and Gallant Hill are a well-matched pair.

赏析

  本诗前五句写画中绝岛，中间四句写画中客舟，末四句为合写，利用民间传说，以戏语结尾，妙趣横生。全诗以画面为线索，一气呵成，但又不拘泥于画面，能充分发挥想象力。[1]

---

1 缪钺等：《宋诗鉴赏辞典》，上海辞书出版社1987年版，第390—391页。

百步洪①二首选一

长洪斗落生跳波，

轻舟南下如投梭。

水师绝叫凫雁②起，

乱石一线争磋磨。

有如兔走鹰隼落，

骏马下注千丈坡。

断弦离柱箭脱手，

飞电过隙珠翻荷。

四山眩转风掠耳，

但见流沫生千涡。

崄中得乐虽一快，

何异水伯夸秋河。

注释

①百步洪：在今徐州市东南二里。②凫雁：野鸭子。

李公麟 画明人行卷（局部） 台北故宫博物院藏

宋 赵佶 写生翎毛卷（局部）台北故宫博物院藏

The Hundred-pace Rapids

Leaping waves grow where the long rapids steeply fall,
A light boat shoots south like a plunging shuttle. Lo!
Waterbirds fly up at the boatman's desperate call.
Among jagged rocks it strives to thread its way and go
As a hare darts away, an eagle dives below,
A gallant steed gallops down a slope beyond control,
A string snaps from a lute, an arrow from a bow,
Lightning cleaves clouds or off lotus leaves raindrops roll.
The mountains whirl around, the wind sweeps by the ear,
I see the current boil in a thousand whirlpools.
At the risk of life I feel a joy without peer,
Unlike the god who boasts of the river he rules.

我生乘化①日夜逝，

坐觉一念逾新罗②。

纷纷争夺醉梦里，

岂信荆棘埋铜驼。

觉来俯仰失千劫③，

回视此水殊委蛇④。

君看岸边苍石上，

古来篙眼如蜂窠。

但应此心无所住，

造物虽驶如吾何！

回船上马各归去，

多言哓哓⑤师所呵。

注释

　　①乘化：顺应自然。②新罗：朝鲜古国名。③千劫：即很长时间。
④委蛇（wēi yí）：转曲自得的样子。⑤哓哓（xiāo）：说个不停。

I give in to changes that take place day and night,

My thoughts can wander far away though I sit here.

Many people in drunken dreams contend and fight.

Do they know palaces 'mid weeds will disappear?

Awakened, they'd regret to have lost a thousand days;

Coming here, they will find the river freely rolls.

If on the riverside rocks you just turn your gaze,

You will see they are honeycombed by the punt-poles.

If your mind from earthly things is detached and freed,

Although nature may change, you'll never be care-worn.

Let us go back or in a boat or on a steed.

Our Abbot will hold this vain argument in scorn.

赏析

　　本诗前半描写水势，后半表达佛教的世界观。二者相联系的媒介是速度。由水速写到"一念""千劫"，水流虽快，但比不上世事变化之快。作者在这里感慨人生有限，宇宙无穷，呼应《赤壁赋》中的"哀吾生之须臾，羡长江之无穷"。[1]

1　缪钺等：《宋诗鉴赏辞典》，上海辞书出版社1987年版，第391—393页。

舟中夜起

微风萧萧吹菰蒲①，

开门看雨月满湖。

舟人水鸟两同梦，

大鱼惊窜如奔狐。

夜深人物不相管，

我独形影相嬉娱。

暗潮生渚②吊③寒蚓④，

落月挂柳看悬蛛。

此生忽忽忧患里，

清境过眼能须臾⑤！

鸡鸣钟动百鸟散，

船头击鼓还相呼。

注释

①菰（gū）蒲：茭白和菖蒲。②渚（zhǔ）：水边。③吊：怜悯。④寒蚓：即蚯蚓。⑤能须臾：如此之快。

Getting up at Night While in a Boat

I take for rain the breeze which rustles through the reed,

Opening the hatch, I find a lake full of moonbeams.

Boatmen and waterbirds share alike the same dreams;

Like scurrying foxes, startled fish away speed.

Man and nature forget each other when night is deep,

Playing alone with my shadow amuses me.

The setting moon like spider hangs from willow tree;

Dark tides creeping over the flats for earthworms weep.

Our life laden with care and spent in worry fleets,

A pure vision before the eyes cannot last long.

Flocks of birds scatter at ringing bells and cock's song,

You'll hear from the prow but boatmen's shout and drumbeats.

赏析

　　本诗描绘了舟中夜起后所观赏到的美丽图画。此六句可分三层，两句一折，写出了 "静" "独" "冷" 三种心境，曲折有致地表露了诗人的心曲情怀。[1]

1　李梦生：《宋诗三百首全解》，复旦大学出版社2007年版，第95—96页。

端午遍游诸寺得禅字

肩舆①任所适，

遇胜辄流连。

焚香引幽步，

酌茗开净筵。

微雨止还作，

小窗幽更妍。

盆山不见日，

草木自苍然。

忽登最高塔②，

眼界穷大千。

卞峰③照城郭，

震泽④浮云天。

注释

①肩舆（yú）：一种用人力抬扛的代步工具。②最高塔：指湖州飞英寺中的飞英塔。③卞（biàn）峰：指卞山，在湖州西北十八里。④震泽：太湖。

Visiting Temples on the Dragon Boat Festival

I go sight-seeing in my sedan-chair
And stop where there's a scenic spot to see.
Burning incense attracts me to go where
I may have vegetable feast and tea.
The gentle rain stops and then starts again,
The little window looks gloomy and clean.
Shut out from sunlight by the hills, the plain
Is overspread with grass and trees so green.
When I ascend the peak'd pagoda, all
The boundless land extends before my eyes.
The Northern Peak o'erlooks the city wall;
On the Lake Zhenze float the cloudy skies.

深沉既可喜，
旷荡亦所便。
幽寻未云毕，
墟落生晚烟。
归来记所历，
耿耿清不眠。
道人亦未寝，
孤灯同夜禅。

A quiet place affords me keen delight;

In space immense I feel under no yoke.

Still looking for some more secluded sight,

I see from villages rise evening smoke.

Come back, I write down my impression deep,

Musing o'er it, I pass a sleepless night.

Nor do the devoted monks take their sleep,

They sit in meditation by lamplight.

赏析

　　本诗描写了湖州五月的景物，并发表了评论。诗人既欣赏太湖的那种吐吸江湖、无所不容的深沉大度，又喜爱登高眺远，景象开阔的旷荡。[1]

1　缪钺等：《宋诗鉴赏辞典》，上海辞书出版社1987年版，第400—401页。

陈季常①所蓄朱陈村嫁娶图二首

一

何年顾陆②丹青手，

画作朱陈嫁娶图。

闻道一村惟两姓，

不将门户买崔卢。

二

我是朱陈旧使君，

劝农曾入杏花村。

而今风物那堪画：

县吏催钱夜打门。

注释

  ①陈季常：名慥，字季常，北宋隐士。②顾陆：顾恺之、陆探微，均为晋代知名画家。

A Picture of Wedding in Zhu-Chen Village

I

A great master of ancient days like Gu or Lu
Painted this picture of wedding of Chen and Zhu.
'Tis said the villagers bear only these two names,
They would not change their household for Cui's and Lu's fames.

II

I came among apricot trees to advocate
Farming in their village when I was magistrate.
But now you can find such picturesque scene no more,
For tax-collectors will nightly knock at the door.

赏析

    前一首诗借古画之意而抒今情，表现诗人对当今封建门阀制度的痛恨。后一首诗描绘重赋苛税带来的沉重灾难，概括出新法的弊端。这两首诗在写法上各有特点，前者照顾题面，勾勒画中之景；后者则在画外做文章，题画而不拘泥于画，两首诗又自成对比，情感自出。[1]

---

1   葛泽溥选评笺释：《苏轼题画诗选评笺释》，河南大学出版社2012年版，第104—109页。

雨晴后，步至四望亭①下渔池上，遂自乾明寺前东冈上归二首

一

雨过浮萍合，

蛙声满四邻。

海棠真一梦，

梅子欲尝新。

挂杖闲挑菜，

秋千不见人。

殷勤木芍药，

独自殿②余春。

二

高亭废已久，

下有种鱼塘。

暮色千山人，

春风百草香。

市桥人寂寂，

古寺竹苍苍。

鹳鹤来何处?

号鸣满夕阳!

注释

①四望亭：在今湖北黄冈。②殿：泛指序列之末。

The Four-view Pavilion

I

Duckweeds meet after the showers,
Frogs are croaking far and near.
Like dreams fade crab-apple flowers,
Yet we may taste fresh plums here.
I carry vegetables, cane in hand,
And see no maiden on the swing.
But pleasing peonies there stand,
Alone they crown departing spring.

II

The high pavilion lies ruined for long,
But below there still remains a fish pond.
In the dusk a thousand hills are drowned;
The spring breeze is sweet with herbs in throng.
The market place appears forlorn;
The old temple with bamboo is green.
Stork and crane come to enliven the scene,
The setting sun is o'erflowed with their horn.

赏析

　　第一首写雨晴后散步所见之景。第二首写步至四望亭下鱼池上，遂自乾明寺东冈上归。这两首诗写景如画，景中有情，旨意含蓄，富有韵味。[1]

1　缪钺等：《宋诗鉴赏辞典》，上海辞书出版社1987年版，第405—407页。

黄州：一蓑烟雨任平生

西江月
黄州中秋

世事一场大梦，
人生几度秋凉。
夜来风叶已鸣廊，
看取眉头鬓上。

酒贱常愁客少，
月明多被云妨。
中秋谁与共孤光？
把盏凄然北望。

The Moon on the West River

Like dreams pass world affairs untold,

How many autumns in our life are cold?

My corridor is loud with wind-blown leaves at night.

See my brows frown and hair turn white!

Of my poor wine few guests are proud;

The bright moon is oft veiled in cloud.

Who would enjoy with me the mid-autumn moon lonely?

Wine cup in hand, northward I look only.

赏析

  本词上片写感伤，寓情于景，咏人生之短促，叹壮志之难酬。下片写悲愤，借景抒情，感世道之险恶，悲人生之寥落。由秋思及人生，触景生情，感慨悲歌，情真意切，令人回味无穷。[1]

---

1 唐圭璋等：《唐宋词鉴赏辞典（唐·五代·北宋）》，上海辞书出版社1988年版，第628—629页。

西江月
顷在黄州

顷在黄州，春夜行蕲水[①]中，过酒家饮；酒醉，乘月至一溪桥上，解鞍曲肱，醉卧，少休；及觉，已晓，乱山攒拥，流水锵然，疑非尘世也。书此语桥柱上。

照野弥弥浅浪，
横空隐隐层霄。
障泥[②]未解玉骢骄，
我欲醉眠芳草。

可惜[③]一溪风月，
莫教踏碎琼瑶。
解鞍欹[④]枕绿杨桥，
杜宇[⑤]一声春晓。

注释

①蕲（qí）水：水名，在黄州附近。②障泥：马鞯，垂于马腹两侧，用于遮挡尘土。③可惜：可爱。④欹：通"倚"，斜靠。⑤杜宇：杜鹃鸟。

The Moon on the West River
Lines Written on a Bridge

Wave on wave glimmers by the river shores;

Sphere on sphere dimly appears in the sky.

Though unsaddled is my white-jade-like horse,

Drunken, asleep in the sweet grass I'll lie.

My horse's hoofs may break, I'm afraid,

The breeze-rippled brook paved by the moon with white jade.

I tether my horse to a green willow

On the bridge and I pillow

My head on my arm till the cuckoo's songs awake

A spring daybreak.

赏析

  上片写词人路上的见闻和醉态，下片写对美好景物的怜惜之情，抒发了作者乐观、豁达的襟怀。全词寓情于景，情景交融，境界空灵浩渺，读来回味无穷。[1]

---

1 唐圭璋等：《唐宋词鉴赏辞典（唐·五代·北宋）》，上海辞书出版社1988年版，第633—635页。

定风波
莫听穿林打叶声

三月七日，沙湖道中遇雨，雨具先去，同行皆狼狈，余独不觉。已而遂晴，故作此。

莫听穿林打叶声。
何妨吟啸且徐行。
竹杖芒鞋轻胜马，
谁怕！
一蓑烟雨任平生。

料峭春风吹酒醒，
微冷。
山头斜照却相迎。
回首向来萧瑟处，
归去。
也无风雨也无晴。

Calming the Waves

Caught in Rain on My Way to the Sandy Lake

On the 7th day of the 3rd month we were caught in rain on our way to the Sandy Lake. The umbrellas had gone ahead, my companions were quite downhearted, but I took no notice. It soon cleared, and I wrote this.

Listen not to the rain beating against the trees.
I had better walk slowly while chanting at ease.
Better than a saddle I like sandals and cane.
I'd fain,
In a straw cloak, spend my life in mist and rain.

Drunken, I am sobered by the vernal wind shrill
And rather chill.
In front, I see the slanting sun atop the hill;
Turning my head, I see the dreary beaten track.
Let me go back!
Impervious to rain or shine, I'll have my own will.

赏析

　　此词通过野外途中偶遇风雨这一生活中的小事，于简朴中见深意，于寻常处生奇景，表现出旷达超脱的胸襟，寄寓着超凡脱俗的人生理想。[1]

1　吴熊和：《唐宋词汇评·两宋卷（一）》，浙江教育出版社2004年版，第443—444页。

浣溪沙

　　游蕲水清泉寺，寺临兰溪①，溪水西流。

山下兰芽短浸溪，
松间沙路净无泥。
萧萧②暮雨子规③啼。

谁道人生无再少？
门前流水尚能西。
休将白发唱黄鸡！

注释

　　①兰溪：蕲水的旧称。②萧萧：形容雨声。③子规：杜鹃鸟。

Silk-washing Stream
Visit to the Temple of Clear Fountain on the West-flowing Stream of Orchid

In the brook below the hill is drowned short orchid bud;
On the sandy path between pine-trees there's no mud.
Shower by shower falls the rain while cuckoos sing.

Who says a man cannot be restored to his spring?
In front of the temple the water still flows west.
Why can't the cock crow at dawn though with a white crest?

赏析

　　本词上阕写暮春三月清泉寺幽雅的风光和环境，下阕抒发使人感奋的议论，表现了作者老当益壮、自强不息的精神。

念奴娇

赤壁怀古

大江东去，

浪淘尽，

千古风流人物。

故垒西边，

人道是、三国周郎赤壁。

乱石崩云，

惊涛拍岸，

卷起千堆雪。

江山如画，

一时多少豪杰。

The Charm of a Maiden Singer
The Red Cliff

The great river eastward flows;
With its waves are gone all those
Gallant heroes of bygone years.
West of the ancient fortress appears
Red Cliff where General Zhou won his early fame
When the Three Kingdoms were in flame.
Rocks tower in the air and waves beat on the shore.
Rolling up a thousand heaps of snow.
To match the land so fair, how many heroes of yore
Had made great show!

遥想公瑾当年，

小乔初嫁了，

雄姿英发。

羽扇纶巾①，

谈笑间、樯橹②灰飞烟灭。

故国神游，

多情应笑我，

早生华发。

人间如梦，

一尊③还酹江月④。

注释

①纶（guān）巾：青丝制成的头巾。②樯（qiáng）橹：代指曹军战船。③尊：通"樽"，酒杯。④还（huán）酹（lèi）江月：指洒酒酹月。

I fancy General Zhou at the height

Of his success, with a plume fan in hand,

In a silk hood, so brave and bright,

Laughing and jesting with his bride so fair,

While enemy ships were destroyed as planned

Like castles in the air.

Should their souls revisit this land,

Sentimental, his bride would laugh to say:

Younger than they, I have my hair turned grey.

Life is but like a dream.

O Moon, I drink to you who have seen them on the stream.

赏析

　　本词借对古代战场的凭吊和对风流人物功业的追念，曲折表达了怀才不遇的忧愤和旷达之心。全词将写景、咏史、抒情融为一体，给人以撼魂荡魄的艺术力量，被誉为"古今绝唱"。[1]

1　唐圭璋等：《唐宋词鉴赏辞典（唐·五代·北宋）》，上海辞书出版社1988年版，第620—623页。

临江仙
夜归临皋^①

夜饮东坡^②醒复醉,

归来仿佛三更。

家童鼻息已雷鸣。

敲门都不应,

倚杖听江声。

长恨此身非我有,

何时忘却营营^③?

夜阑风静縠纹^④平。

小舟从此逝,

江海寄余生。

注释

①临皋(gāo):即临皋亭。②东坡:在湖北黄冈县东。③营营:形容内心躁急。④縠(hú)纹:比喻水波细纹。

Riverside Daffodils
Returning to Lingao by Night

Drinking at Eastern Slope by night,

I sober, then get drunk again.

When I come back, it seems to be mid-night.

I hear the thunder of my houseboy's snore,

I knock but none answers the door.

What can I do but, leaning on my cane,

Listen to the river's refrain?

I long regret I am not master of my own.

When can I ignore the hums of up and down?

In the still night the soft winds quiver

On the ripples of the river.

From now on, I would vanish with my little boat,

For the rest of my life, on the sea I would float.

赏析

  本词上阕叙事，着意渲染其醉态，下阕就写酒醒时的思想活动。全词写景、叙事、抒情、议论水乳交融，不假雕饰，语言畅达，格调超逸，颇能体现苏词特色。[1]

---

1 唐圭璋等：《唐宋词鉴赏辞典（唐·五代·北宋）》，上海辞书出版社1988年版，第640—641页。

卜算子
黄州定慧院^①寓居作

缺月挂疏桐，

漏断人初静。

谁见幽人独往来？

缥缈孤鸿影。

惊起却回头，

有恨无人省。

拣尽寒枝不肯栖，

寂寞沙洲冷。

注释

① 定慧院：在今湖北省黄冈市东南。苏轼初贬黄州，寓居于此。

Song of Divination
Written at Dinghui Abbey in Huangzhou

From a sparse plane tree hangs the waning moon,
The waterclock is still and hushed is man.
Who sees a hermit pacing up and down alone?
Is it the shadow of a fugifive swan?

Startled, he turns his head
With a grief none behold.
Looking all over, he won't perch on branches dead
But on the lonely sandbank cold.

赏析

　　本词上阕写鸿见人，下阕写人见鸿，借月夜孤鸿这一形象托物寓怀，表达了词人蔑视流俗的心境。

南乡子
重九^①涵辉楼^②呈徐君猷^③

霜降水痕收^④，

浅碧鳞鳞露远洲。

酒力渐消风力软，

飕飕，

破帽多情却恋头。

佳节若为酬^⑤，

但把清樽断送秋。

万事到头都是梦，

休休^⑥，

明日黄花蝶也愁。

注释

　　①重九：农历九月初九重阳节。②涵辉楼：在黄冈县西南。③徐君猷（yóu）：名大受，当时黄州知州。④水痕收：指水位降低。⑤若为酬：怎样应付过去。⑥休休：不要，此处意旨不要再提往事。

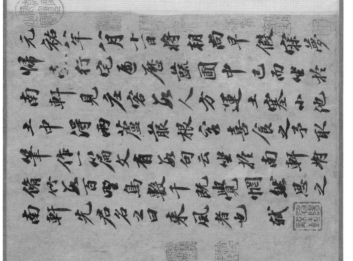

宋 苏轼 书南轩梦语 台北故宫博物院藏

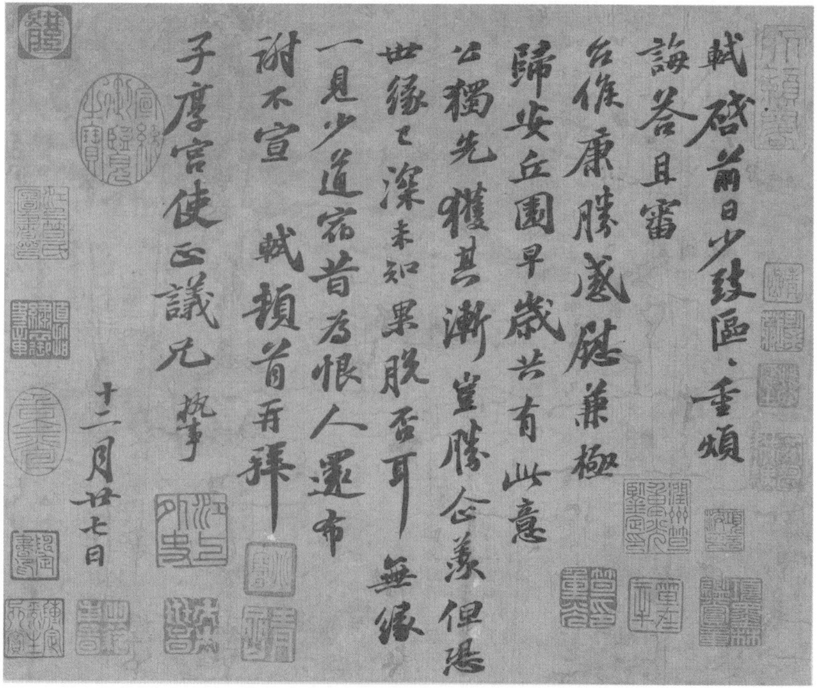

宋 苏轼 致子厚宫使正议尺牍 台北故宫博物院藏

Song of Southern Country
To Governor Xu on Mountain-climbing Day

The tide flows out after the fall of frost,

From rippling green water a beach of sand will rise.

The soughing wind softens, the vigor of wine is lost,

When blows the breeze,

My sympathetic hat won't leave my head with ease,

How shall we pass the holiday?

Wine cup in hand, we may send autumn away.

Everything will end in dreams,

It seems

Tomorrow fallen blooms will sadden butterflies.

赏析

  词上片写登临远望之所观所感，下片借登高宴饮来抒发自己达观的人生态度。全词使用戏谑的手法，抒发了词人旷达乐观而又略带惆怅的矛盾心境。[1]

1　林力、肖剑主编：《宋词鉴赏大典（上、中、下卷）》，长征出版社1999年版，第316—317页。

鹧鸪天

林断山明①竹隐墙。

乱蝉衰草小池塘。

翻空白鸟时时见，

照水红蕖②细细香。

村舍外，古城傍。

杖藜徐步转斜阳。

殷勤昨夜三更雨，

又得浮生一日凉。

注释

①林断山明：树林断绝处，山峰显现出来。②红蕖（qú）：荷花。

Partridges in the Sky
One More Fresh Day

Through forest breaks appear hills and bamboo-screened wall,

Cicadas shrill o'er withered grass near a pool small.

White birds are seen now and then looping in the air;

Pink lotus blooms on lake-side exude fragrance spare.

Beyond the cots,

Near the old town,

Cane in hand, I stroll round while the sun's slanting down.

Thanks to the welcome rain which fell when night was deep,

Now in my floating life one more fresh day I reap.

赏析

　　本词上片写景，下片刻画人物形象，描绘了一幅夏日雨后的农村小景，抒发了作者雨后得新凉的喜悦，也展现出一个抑郁不得志的隐者形象。[1]

1　唐圭璋等：《唐宋词鉴赏辞典（唐·五代·北宋）》，上海辞书出版社1988年版，第643—644页。

满庭芳

　　有王长官^①者，弃官黄州三十三年，黄人谓之王先生。因送陈慥^②来过余，因为赋此。

三十三年，

今谁存者？

算只君与长江。

凛然苍桧^③，

霜干苦难双。

闻道司州古县，

云溪上、竹坞松窗。

江南^④岸，

不因送子^⑤，

宁肯过吾邦？

注释

　　①王长官：苏轼好友，名字与事迹不详。②陈慥（zào）：字季常，苏轼好友。③桧：即圆柏。④江南：黄陂在黄州西北，长江横亘其间，故黄州于黄陂可称江南。⑤子：指陈慥。

Courtyard Full of Fragrance

After thirty-three years.
Who still remains today?
Only you and the long, long river stay.
Upright like the cypress evergreen,
Frost-proof, you have no compeers.
In your old county I have seen
Your cot surrounded by bamboos
Standing by cloudy stream framed with pine tree on tree.
If you leave the southern shore not to say adieus,
How could you come to see me?

摐摐①，

疏雨过，

风林舞破，

烟盖云幢。

愿持此邀君，

一饮空缸。

居士先生老矣，

真梦里、相对残釭②。

歌声断，

行人未起，

船鼓已逢逢③。

注释

①摐（chuāng）摐：形容雨声。②釭（gāng）：灯。③逢（péng）逢：此处指开船的信号。

After a sudden shower the trees

Dance in the breeze,

A veil of mist rises with cloud screen.

I hold high the wine cup

And invite you to drink it up.

Now old, I think it's like a dream sweet

To drink face to face with you.

We hear no more songs of adieu,

For early risers, drums begin to beat.

赏析

　　本词着力刻画王长官卓异的高士形象，抒写与其倾盖如故的情怀。全词将叙事、写人、状景、抒情打成一片，既写一方奇人之品格，又抒旷达豪放之情感。词中凛然如苍桧的王先生这一形象，可谓东坡理想人格追求的绝妙写照。[1]

1　唐圭璋等：《唐宋词鉴赏辞典（唐·五代·北宋）》，上海辞书出版社1988年版，第604—607页。

满庭芳

蜗角虚名，

蝇头微利，

算来著甚干忙①？

事皆前定，

谁弱又谁强？

且趁闲身未老，

须放我、些子②疏狂！

百年里，

浑教是醉，

三万六千场。

注释

    ①著甚干忙：白忙什么。②些子：一点儿。

Courtyard Full of Fragrance

For fame as vain as a snail's horn
And profit as slight as a fly's head,
Should I be busy and forlorn?
Fate rules for long,
Who is weak? Who is strong?
Not yet grown old and having leisure,
Let me be free to enjoy pleasure!
Could I be drunk in a hundred years,
Thirty-six hundred times without shedding tears?

思量，

能几许，

忧愁风雨，

一半相妨。

又何须，

抵死说短论长？

幸对清风皓月，

苔茵①展、云幕高张。

江南好，

千钟②美酒，

一曲满庭芳。

注释

　　①苔茵：如褥的草地。②钟：即"盅"，酒器。

Think how long life can last,

Though sad and harmful storms I've passed.

Why should I waste my breath

Until my death,

To say the short and long

Or right and wrong?

I am happy to enjoy clear breeze and the moon bright,

Green grass outspread

And a canopy of cloud white.

The Southern shore is fine

With a thousand cups of wine

And the courtyard fragrant with song.

赏析

　　本词上片由讽世到愤世，下片从自叹到自适，展示了作者人生道路上受到重大挫折之后既愤世嫉俗又飘逸旷达的内心世界，表现了作者宠辱皆忘、超然物外的人生态度。[1]

1　刘石评注：《苏轼词选》，人民文学出版社2015年版，第190—192页。

满庭芳
留别雪堂①

归去来兮，

吾归何处？

万里家在岷峨②。

百年强半，

来日苦无多。

坐见黄州再闰，

儿童尽、吴语楚歌。

山中友，

鸡豚社酒，

相劝老东坡。

注释

　　①雪堂：苏轼在黄州的居所名。②岷峨（mín é）：四川的岷山与峨眉山，此代指作者故乡。

Courtyard Full of Fragrance
Leaving My Hall of Snow

Why not go home?

Where shall I go today?

My home in Eyebrow Mountain is thousand miles away.

Fifty years old, I have not many days to come.

Living here for four years,

My children sing the Southern song.

Villagers and mountaineers

With meat and wine ask me to stay

In Eastern Slope for long.

云何？

当此去，

人生底事，

来往如梭。

待闲看，

秋风洛水清波。

好在堂前细柳，

应念我、莫剪柔柯①。

仍传语，

江南父老，

时与晒渔蓑！

注释

　　①柔柯（kē）：指柳条。

What shall I say

When I've left here?

How will my life appear?

Just as a shuttle comes and goes.

At leisure I'll see autumn breeze blows

And ripples the river clear,

I'll think of my willow tree slender.

Will you trim for me its twigs tender?

Please tell Southern villagers not to forget

To bask my straw cloak and fishing net!

赏析

  本词上片抒写对蜀中故里的思念和对黄州邻里父老的惜别之情，下片进一步将宦途失意之怀与留恋黄州之意对写，突出了作者达观豪放的性格。[1]

---

1 王思宇：《苏轼精品词赏析集》，巴蜀书社1996年版，第240—245页。

虞美人

波声拍枕长淮①晓，

隙月②窥人小。

无情汴水③自东流，

只载一船离恨、向西州④。

竹溪⑤花浦曾同醉，

酒味多于泪。

谁教风鉴⑥在尘埃，

酝造一场烦恼、送人来!

注释

  ①长淮：指淮水。②隙月：船蓬缝里露出来的月亮。③汴水：源于河南，入淮河。④西州：指东晋时扬州公廨的西门。⑤竹溪：借唐代"竹溪六逸"喻指作者与秦观之间的交游。⑥风鉴：指风度识见。

The Beautiful Lady Yu

River Huai's waves seem to beat my pillow till dawn;
A ray of moonbeam peeps at me forlorn.
The heartless River Bian flows eastward down,
Laden with parting grief, you've left the town.

Once we got drunk by riverside bamboo and flower,
My tears made sweet wine sour.
How could a mirror not be stained with dust?
Who could predict the trouble brewing up in gust?

赏析

　　词上片咏东坡与秦观夜饮于舟中，感叹人生，下片叙与秦观难忘情分，惜秦观贤才埋没，抒发人生短暂和壮志难酬的愁绪。[1]

1　刘默等编著：《宋词鉴赏大全集 上》，中国华侨出版社2012年版，第171页。

调笑令

渔父，

渔父，

江上微风细雨。

青蓑黄箬①裳衣②，

红酒白鱼暮归。

归暮，

归暮，

长笛一声何处？

注释

　①箬（ruò）：竹壳。②裳（cháng）衣：下身服饰。

Song of Flirtation

Fisherman,

Fisherman,

On the river in gentle wind and rain,

In blue straw cloak, broad-brimmed hat on the head,

He comes back late at dusk with fish white and wine red.

Come late with ease,

Come late with ease,

He plays his flute, but who knows where he is?

赏析

  全词运用对仗、叠句、偏正词，颠倒词等写作手法，描绘了一幅渔父田园江湖生活的图景，表达了苏轼对渔父的羡慕之情，以及对隐居生活的向往。[1]

---

1 朱靖华等 :《苏轼词新释辑评》，中国书店出版社2010年版，第865—866页。

洞仙歌
花蕊夫人

　　仆七岁时，见眉州老尼，姓朱，忘其名，年九十岁。自言尝随其师入蜀主孟昶①宫中。一日大热，蜀主与花蕊夫人②夜纳凉摩诃池上，作一词。朱具③能记之。今四十年，朱已死久矣，人无知此词者。但记其首两句。暇日寻味，岂洞仙歌令乎？乃为足之云。

冰肌玉骨，
自清凉无汗。
水殿风来暗香满。
绣帘开、一点明月窥人。
人未寝，
欹枕钗横鬓乱。

注释

　　①孟昶：五代时蜀国君主。②花蕊夫人：孟昶的妃子。③具：通"俱"，全，都。

Song of a Fairy in the Cave
Madame Pistil

*When I was seven, a ninety-year-old nun told me that she had visited the
palace of King Meng Chang, where she saw, on a sweltering hot night, the
king and his favorite wife Madame Pistil sitting in the shade by a big pool,
writing a poem, which she could still recite. Now forty years have passed.
As the nun died long ago, nobody knows that poem now. I still remember
the first two lines and think it is perhaps written to the tune of the "Song
of a Fairy in the Cave". So I complete Meng Chang's poem as follows:*

Your jade-like bones and ice-like skin
Are naturally sweatless, fresh and cool.
The breeze brings the unperceivable fragrance in
And fills the bower by the pool.
The embroidered screen rolled up lets in
A bright spot of a moon which peeps at you there
Leaning on the pillow, not asleep, a hairpin
Across your dishevelled hair.

起来携素手，

庭户无声，

时见疏星渡河汉。

试问夜如何？

夜已三更，

金波①淡、玉绳②低转。

但屈指、西风几时来，

又不道流年，

暗中偷换。

注释

　　①金波：指月光。②玉绳：星名。

We two rise hand in hand,

Silent in the courtyard we stand.

At times we see shooting stars stray

Across the Milky Way.

How old has night become?

The watchmen thrice have beaten the drum.

The golden moonbeams begin to fade,

Low is the Big Dipper's string of jade.

We count on our fingers when the west wind will blow.

What can we do with years which drift as rivers flow?

赏析

　　本词描述了五代时后蜀国君孟昶与其妃花蕊夫人夏夜在摩诃池上纳凉的情景，着意刻绘了花蕊夫人姿质与心灵的美好、高洁，表达了词人对时光流逝的深深惋惜和感叹。[1]

1　唐圭璋等：《唐宋词鉴赏辞典（唐·五代·北宋）》，上海辞书出版社1988年版，第674—676页。

洞仙歌

咏柳

江南腊尽，

早梅花开后，

分付①新春与垂柳。

细腰肢、自有入格风流。

仍更是，

骨体清英雅秀。

永丰坊②那畔，

尽日无人，

谁见金丝③弄晴昼？

断肠④是、飞絮时，

绿叶成阴，

无个事、一成⑤消瘦，

又莫是、东风逐君来，

便吹散眉间，

一点春皱。

注释

①分付：付托，寄意。②永丰坊：地名，在洛阳。③金丝：比喻柳树的垂条。④断肠：秋海棠花的别称。⑤一成：宋时口语，同"渐渐"。

Song of a Fairy in the Cave
The Willow Tree

In the end of the year on Southern shore

When early mume blossoms disappear,

The newcome spring dwells on the weeping willow tree,

Its slender waist reveals a personality free,

And what is more,

Its trunk appears more elegant and freer.

Along the way

There are no sight-seers all the day.

Who'd come to see your golden thread in sunlight sway?

Your heart would break to see catkins fly,

Your green leaves make a shade of deep dye.

Having nothing to do,

You would grow thinner, too.

If you come again with vernal breeze now,

It would dispel the vernal grief on your brow.

赏析

　　本词上片写柳的体态标格和风韵之美，下片转入对垂柳不幸遭遇的感叹，以含蓄婉曲的手法和饱含感情的笔调，借婀娜多姿、落寞失时的垂柳，流露出作者对女性深切的同情与赞美。[1]

1　唐圭璋等：《唐宋词鉴赏辞典（唐·五代·北宋）》，上海辞书出版社1988年版，第672—674页。

红梅

怕愁贪睡独开迟，
自恐冰容不入时。
故作小红桃杏色，
尚余孤瘦雪霜姿。
寒心未肯随春态，
酒晕无端上玉肌。
诗老不知梅格在，
更看绿叶与青枝。

Red Mume Blossom

Enjoying sleep and shunning sadness, she blossoms late,

Afraid an icy look might not be up to date.

Like peach and apricot she rouges her fair face;

Like snow and frost she has her lonely, slender grace.

Her heart is cold and will not seek to please as spring;

Her skin like jade is tinged with the hue wine would bring.

How can she be described? An old poet knows not

But says she's leafless peach and green-boughed apricot.

赏析

　　本诗托物言志，以红梅傲然挺立的品格，抒发了自己达观超脱的襟怀和不愿随波逐流的傲骨。

正月二十日与潘、郭二生^①出郊寻春，忽记去年是日同至女王城^②作诗，乃和前韵

东风未肯入东门，

走马还寻去岁村。

人似秋鸿来有信，

事如春梦了无痕。

江城白酒三杯釅^③，

野老苍颜一笑温。

已约年年为此会，

故人不用赋招魂。

注释

①潘郭二生：苏轼在黄州的朋友潘大临和郭遘。②女王城：即黄州州治东十五里的永安城。③釅（yàn）：液汁很浓。

Seeking Spring

Seeking spring with two friends on the 20th day of the 1st lunar month reminded me of the poem written on the same day last year, and I wrote these lines in the same rhymes.

The east wind will not enter the east gate with glee,

I ride to seek the village visited last year.

Old friends still ask autumn swans to bring word to me;

The bygones like spring dreams have left no traces here.

Three cups of strong wine by riverside keep us late;

A smile of the grey-haired countryman warms my heart.

Each year we will meet here on an appointed date,

It's useless for my friends to hasten my depart.

赏析

本诗写寻春之乐，同时抒发了"人如秋鸿，事如春梦"的感叹，用人生虚无的思想来排遣心中的烦恼和痛苦，最后两句则表达了诗人豁达的襟怀。此诗对仗精妙，比喻新颖，把抽象的事物塑造得美妙具体，大大增强了艺术效果。[1]

1　缪钺等：《宋诗鉴赏辞典》，上海辞书出版社2015年版，第446—448页。

春日

鸣鸠乳燕寂无声，
日射西窗泼眼明。
午醉醒来无一事，
只将春睡赏春晴。

Spring Day

Cooing pigeons and nursling swallows weave no cries,
Sunlight piercing western windows dazzles the eyes.
Awakened from noonday torpor, indolent I stay,
And enjoy in my spring sleep a sunny spring day.

赏析

　　本诗描写作者在春日里百无聊赖，喝酒昏睡，浑浑噩噩度日的情景，从而流露出遭人谗害排挤，有志难逞，年华虚度的无奈。

寒食雨二首

一

自我来黄州，

已过三寒食，

年年欲惜春，

春去不容惜。

今年又苦雨，

两月秋萧瑟，

卧闻海棠花，

泥污燕脂雪①。

暗中偷负去，

夜半真有力。

何殊病少年，

病起头已白。

注释

　①燕脂雪：指海棠花瓣。

宋 佚名 宋人著人春会图卷（局部） 台北故宫博物院藏

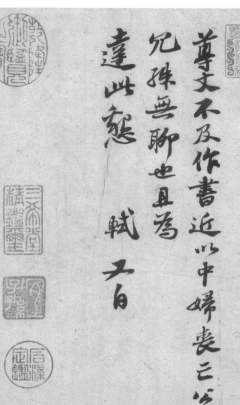

尊文不及作書近以中婦喪亡心私紛兄孫無聊也且為達此懃賦五日

宋 苏轼 书尺牍 台北故宫博物院藏

Rain at the Cold-food Festival

I

Since I came to Huangzhou, I've passed
Three Cold-food days devot'd to fast.
Each year I wish fair spring to stay,
But spring will go without delay.
This year again we suffer from rains,
For two months dreary autumn reigns.
Lying in bed, I smell crab-apple flowers,
Upon whose rouge and snow mud showers.
The rouge has taken stealthy flight,
Borne away by the Strong at midnight.
The snow is like a sick youth's head
Turning white when he's up from his bed.

二

春江欲入户，

雨势来不已，

小屋如渔舟，

濛濛①水云里。

空庖②煮寒菜③，

破灶烧湿苇。

那知是寒食？

但见乌衔纸。

君门深九重，

坟墓在万里。

也拟哭途穷，

死灰吹不起！

注释

　　①濛濛：雨迷茫的样子。②庖（páo）：厨房。③寒菜：泛指冬天的菜。

II

Spring flood is coming up to my gate,

My small cot looks like a fishing boat.

The pouring rain will not abate,

My cot on misty waves will float.

I cook food in a kitchen in decay

And burn wet reeds in a cracked stove.

Who can tell 'tis the Cold-food day

But for the money-paper burned above?

The royal palace has gate on gate;

My household graves far away lie.

At the road's end I'd lament my fate,

But dead ashes blown up cannot fly.

赏析

  第一首诗描写淫雨、海棠之景，抒发了贬徒身世之情。第二首诗将寒食节的文化意象与作者的身世遭遇结合。两首诗反映出苏轼谪居黄州时痛苦、压抑甚至是绝望的心理状态，以及理想与现实之间激烈的矛盾冲突。[1]

---

1 王水照、朱刚：《苏轼诗词文选评》，上海古籍出版社2004年，第107—108页。

次荆公韵

骑驴渺渺入荒陂^①，

想见先生未病时。

劝我试求三亩宅，

从公已觉十年迟。

注释

①陂（bēi）：山坡。

Reply to Wang Anshi, Former Prime Minister

Riding an ass, I come from afar to visit you,

Still imagining you as healthy as I knew.

You advise me to buy a house at your next gate,

I'd like to follow you, but it is ten years late.

赏析

　　宋神宗元丰七年秋，苏轼赴汝州上任途中路经金陵，逗留月余。时王安石二次罢相后退居金陵，与苏轼相见后唱和颇多。两人虽在政见上观点相左，但在文学和私交上却彼此欣赏并相得甚欢。[1]

1　缪钺等：《宋诗鉴赏辞典》，上海辞书出版社1987年版，第1472—1473页。

题西林壁

横看成岭侧成峰，
远近高低各不同。
不识庐山真面目，
只缘身在此山中。

Written on the Wall at West Forest Temple

It's a range viewed in face and peaks viewed from the side,
Assuming different shapes viewed from far and wide.
Of Mountain Lu we cannot make out the true face,
For we are lost in the heart of the very place.

赏析

　　本诗前两句描述了庐山不同的形态变化，后两句写出了作者深思后的感悟——只有跳出庐山的遮蔽，才能全面把握庐山的真正仪态。全诗借助庐山的形象，用通俗的语言深入浅出地表达哲理，故而亲切自然，耐人寻味。[1]

1　缪钺等：《宋诗鉴赏辞典》，上海辞书出版社1987年版，第420—421页。

琴诗

若言琴上有琴声，
放在匣中何不鸣？
若言声在指头上，
何不于君指上听？

Song of the Lute

If you say music from the lute does rise,

Why in its case will not vibrate its string?

If you say the sound in the fingers lies,

Why have we never heard the fingers sing?

赏析

　　本诗用了两个设问句来启迪人们：有好的琴，又有琴师高超的弹技，才能演奏出动听的曲调。全诗运用了散文句式，诗味虽然不太浓，但诗中的理趣却弥补了它的不足，仍然是耐人寻味的诗，多少体现了宋诗的特征。[1]

1　殷光熹：《宋诗名篇赏析》，北京十月文艺出版社1992年版，第127—128页。

南堂①五首选二

一

江上西山②半隐堤，

此邦③台馆一时西。

南堂独有西南向，

卧看千帆落浅溪。

二

扫地焚香闭阁眠，

簟④纹如水帐如烟。

客来梦觉知何处？

挂起西窗浪接天。

注释

　　①南堂：在临皋亭，俯临长江，是作者贬谪黄州后居住的地方。②西山：即樊山，在今湖北武昌西，与赤壁隔江相对，上有苏圆，为苏轼贬居黄州时的读书处。③此邦：指黄州。④簟（diàn）：竹席。

The Southern Hall

I

The western hills are half hidden by river banks,
All the pavilions of this country face the west.
The Southern Hall has windows on the south and west flanks,
Abed, I see a thousand sails and waves with white crest.

II

Floor swept, incense burning and doors closed, I lie flat
In a mist-like curtain on a ripple-marked mat.
When a guest comes, I wake and wonder where am I,
West windows propp'd open, I see waves meet the sky.

赏析

　　这组诗围绕置身于南堂的种种感受而写，组成一幅精美的山水人物画，表现了清静而壮美的自然环境，表达了悠闲自得的感情，创造出一种清幽绝俗的意境。[1]

1　缪钺等：《宋诗鉴赏辞典》，上海辞书出版社1987年版，第413—415页。

海棠

东风袅袅泛崇光①，
香雾空濛月转廊。
只恐夜深花睡去，
故烧高烛照红妆。

注释

①崇光：高贵华美的光泽。

Crab-apple Flower

The flower in east wind exhales a tender light
And spreads a fragrant mist when the moon turns away.
I am afraid she'd fall asleep at dead of night;
A candle's lit to make her look fair as by day.

赏析

　　本诗首句写白天的海棠，第二句写夜间的海棠，后两句用典故，不仅是把花比作人，也是把人比作花，为花着想，十分感人，表明了作者是一个性情中人，极富浪漫色彩。[1]

1　缪钺等：《宋诗鉴赏辞典》，上海辞书出版社1987年版，第419—420页。

归宜兴留题竹西寺①

此生已觉都无事，

今岁仍逢大有年。

山寺归来闻好语，

野花啼鸟亦欣然。

注释

　　①竹西寺：在扬州。

Written in Zhuxi Temple
on My Way Back to Yixing

The crop still bears a plentiful harvest this year,
I feel myself already free from worldly care.
On my way back from the Temple good news I hear,
Even wild flowers and song birds have a cheerful air.

赏析

　　本诗以轻松的笔调抒发了作者从贬谪中获得解脱的闲适情怀，以及实现归隐心愿的喜悦之情。

惠崇①春江晚景二首

一

竹外桃花三两枝，

春江水暖鸭先知。

蒌蒿②满地芦芽短，

正是河豚欲上时。

二

两两归鸿欲破群，

依依还似北归人。

遥知朔漠多风雪，

更待江南半月春。

注释

①惠崇：福建建阳僧。②蒌蒿：草名。

River Scenes on a Spring Evening Written to Accompany Two Pictures Drawn by Monk Huichong

I

Behind bamboo two or three sprays of peach-tree grow,

When spring has warmed the stream, ducks are the first to know.

The land o'verrun by weeds and water studd'd with reeds,

It is time when globefish to swim upstream preceeds.

II

Returning wild geese from the flock would break away,

North-going wayfarers are reluctant to go.

Knowing from afar the desert's still covered with snow,

For half a month more in the South they would fain stay.

赏析

　　第一首诗题"鸭戏图"，再现了原画中的江南仲春景色，又融入诗人合理的想象，与原画相得益彰。第二首诗题"飞雁图"，对大雁北飞融入人的感情，侧面表现了江南春美。[1]

1　缪钺等：《宋诗鉴赏辞典》，上海辞书出版社1987年版，第429—430页。

京都：一朵红云捧玉皇

水龙吟

次韵^①章质夫^②杨花词

似花还似非花，

也无人惜从教^③坠。

抛家傍路，

思量却是，

无情有思。

萦损柔肠，

困酣^④娇眼，

欲开还闭。

梦随风万里，

寻郎去处，

又还被、莺呼起。

注释

①次韵：用原作之韵，并按照原作用韵次序进行创作。②章质夫：即章楶，建州浦城人。③从教：任凭。④困酣：困倦至极。

Water Dragon's Chant
Willow Catkins

After Zhang Zhifu's lyric on willow catkins, using the same rhyming
words.

They seem to be and not to be flowers,
None pity them when they fall in showers.
Deserting home,
By the roadside they roam;
I think they have no feeling to impart,
But they must have thoughts deep.
Grief numbs their tender heart,
Their wistful eyes heavy with sleep,
About to open, yet closed again.
They dream of going with the wind for long,
Long miles to find a tender-hearted man,
But are aroused by the orioles' song.

不恨此花飞尽，

恨西园、落红难缀。

晓来雨过，

遗踪何在？

一池萍碎。

春色三分，

二分尘土，

一分流水。

细看来，

不是杨花点点，

是离人泪。

I do not grieve willow catkins have flown away,

But that in Western Garden the fallen red

Cannot be gathered. When dawns the day

And rain is o'er, we cannot find their traces

But a pond with broken duckweeds o'erspread.

Of spring's three graces,

Two have gone with the roadside dust,

And one with the waves. If you just

Take a close look, you will never

Find catkins but tears of those who sever,

Which drop by drop

Fall without stop.

赏析　本词主要写杨花飘忽不定的际遇。全词采用拟人的艺术手法，把咏物与写人巧妙地结合起来，真正做到了"借物以寓性情"，写得声韵谐婉，情调幽怨缠绵，反映了苏词婉约的一面。[1]

1　唐圭璋等 :《唐宋词鉴赏辞典（唐·五代·北宋）》，上海辞书出版社1988年版，第597—600页。

贺新郎

乳燕飞华屋。

悄无人、桐阴转午。

晚凉新浴。

手弄生绡①白团扇，

扇手一时似玉。

渐困倚、孤眠清熟②。

帘外谁来推绣户？

枉教人、梦断瑶台曲。

又却是，

风敲竹。

注释

①生绡（xiāo）：这里指丝绢。②清熟：谓睡眠安稳沉酣。

Congratulations to the Bridegroom
The Beauty and the Pomegranate Flower

Young swallows fly along the painted eave,
Which none perceive.
The shade of plane trees keeps away
The hot noonday
And brings an evening fresh and cool
For the bathing lady beautiful.
She flirts a round fan of silk made,
Both fan and hand as white as jade.
Tired by and by,
She falls asleep with lonely sigh.
Who's knocking at the curtained door
That she can dream sweet dreams no more?
It's again the breeze who
Is swaying green bamboo.

石榴半吐红巾蹙①。

待浮花、浪蕊都尽，

伴君幽独。

秾艳②一枝细看取，

芳心千重似束。

又恐被、秋风惊绿。

若待得君来向此，

花前对酒不忍触。

共粉泪，

两簌簌。

注释

①红巾蹙：形容石榴花半开时如红巾皱缩。②秾（nóng）艳：色彩
艳丽。

The pomegranate flower opens half her lips

Which look like wrinkled crimson strips;

When all the wanton flowers fade,

Alone she'll be the beauty's maid.

How charming is her blooming branch, behold!

Her fragrant heart seems wrapped a thousand fold.

But she's afraid to be surprised by western breeze

Which withers all the green leaves on the trees.

The beauty comes to drink to the flower fair;

To see her withered too she cannot bear.

Then tears and flowers

Would fall in showers.

赏析

　　本词上片以初夏景物为衬托，写一位孤高绝尘的美丽女子。下片写伊人观赏榴花，对花落泪，相思断肠。全词以婉曲缠绵的情韵，含蓄表达了作者的情怀，言尽意远，韵味无穷。[1]

1　唐圭璋等：《唐宋词鉴赏辞典（唐·五代·北宋）》，上海辞书出版社1988年版，第670—672页。

鹊桥仙
七夕送陈令举

缑山^①仙子，

高情云渺，

不学痴牛騃女^②。

凤箫声断月明中，

举手谢、时人欲去。

客槎^③曾犯，

银河波浪，

尚带天风海雨。

相逢一醉是前缘，

风雨散、飘然何处？

注释

　　①缑（gōu）山：在今河南偃师县。②痴（chī）牛騃（ái）女：指牛
郎织女。③槎（chá）：竹筏。

Immortal at the Magpie Bridge
Farewell on Double Seventh Eve

Like the immortal leaving the crowd,

Wafting above the cloud,

Unlike the Cowherd and the Maid who fond remain,

You blow your flute in moonlight,

Waving your hand, you go in flight.

Your boat will go away

Across the Milky Way,

In celestial wind and rain.

We've met and drunk as if by fate.

Where will you waft when wind and rain abate?

赏析

　　本词上阕写七夕之事，为友人离别之愁思开怀。下阕则借晋人遇仙的典故表达与友人聚会的快乐和离别的感慨。全词格调上用飘逸超旷取代缠绵悱恻之风，读起来清晰明快，韵味十足。[1]

1　［宋］苏轼：《豪放词》，万卷出版社2018年版，第131页。

八声甘州

寄参寥子^①

有情风、万里卷潮来，

无情送潮归。

问钱塘江上，

西兴^②浦口，

几度斜晖？

不用思量今古，

俯仰昔人非。

谁似东坡老，

白首忘机^③？

注释

　　①参寥子：即僧人道潜，字参寥。精通佛典，工诗，苏轼与之交厚。
②西兴：即西陵，在今杭州萧山区之西。③忘机：忘却世俗的机诈之心。

Eight Beats of Ganzhou Song
For a Buddhist Friend

The heart-stirring breeze brings in the tidal bore;

The heartless wind sees it flow out from river shore.

At the river's mouth

Or the ferry south,

How many times have we heard parting chimes?

Don't grieve over the past!

The world changes fast.

Who could be like me,

Though white-haired, yet carefree?

记取西湖西畔，

正春山好处，

空翠烟霏。

算诗人相得，

如我与君稀。

约他年、东还海道，

愿谢公①、雅志②莫相违。

西州路，

不应回首，

为我沾衣。

注释

①谢公：指谢安。②雅志：很早立下的志愿。

Do not forsake the western shore of the lake:

On fine day the vernal hills are green;

On rainy day they are veiled by misty screen.

Few poets would be

Such bosom friends as you and me.

Do not forget in our old age,

We'll live together in hermitage.

Even if I should disappear,

You should not turn to weep for your compeer.

赏析

    本词上下阕均以写景发端，议论继后。全词以平实的语言，抒写深厚的情意，气势雄放，意境浑然，表现出词人超然物外的人生态度和寄情山水的人生理想。[1]

1   刘怀荣等：《唐宋元诗词曲名篇解读》，济南出版社2003年版，第175—177页。

临江仙
送钱穆父①

一别都门②三改火，

天涯踏尽红尘。

依然一笑作春温。

无波真古井，

有节是秋筠③。

惆怅孤帆连夜发，

送行淡月微云。

尊前不用翠眉④颦⑤。

人生如逆旅⑥，

我亦是行人。

注释

①钱穆父：即钱勰，苏轼友人。②都门：指都城的城门。③筠（yún）：竹子的青皮，借指竹子。④翠眉：古代妇女的一种眉饰。⑤颦（pín）：皱眉。⑥逆旅：旅舍。

Riverside Daffodils
Farewell to a Friend

Three years have passed since we left the capital;

We've trodden all the way from rise to fall.

Still I smile as on warm spring day.

In ancient well no waves are raised;

Upright, the autumn bamboo's praised.

Melancholy, your lonely sail departs at night;

Only a pale cloud sees you off in pale moonlight.

You need no songstress to drink your sorrow away.

Life is like a journey;

I too am on my way.

赏析

    此词上片写与友人久别重聚，下片写月夜与友人分别，抒发了词人对世事人生的超旷之思。感情一波三折，委曲跌宕，写的可谓动人心弦。[1]

---

1   唐圭璋等：《唐宋词鉴赏辞典（唐·五代·北宋）》，上海辞书出版社1988年版，第639—640页。

书李世南①所画秋景

野水参差落涨痕，

疏林欹倒出霜根。

扁舟一棹归何处？

家在江南黄叶村。

注释

　①李世南：宋代著名画家，工画山水。

Autumn Scene Written to Accompany a Picture Drawn by Li Shinan

Creeks crisscross the meadow, banks scarred where water rose;
Sparse trees slant and let their frost-bitten roots stick out.
Do you know where the single-oared, leaf-like boat goes?
To the village of yellow leaves or thereabout.

赏析

　　本诗前二句以浓笔勾勒景物，后二句发挥想象，表现悠扬情调。全诗情调高远，意趣丰富，神思驰骋，翻空出奇，给读者以美的享受。[1]

1　缪钺等：《宋诗鉴赏辞典》，上海辞书出版社1987年版，第433—434页。

书鄢陵①王主簿②所画折枝③二首

一

论画以形似，

见与儿童邻。

赋诗必此诗，

定非知诗人。

诗画本一律，

天工与清新。

边鸾雀写生，

赵昌花传神。

何如此两幅，

疏淡含精匀！

谁言一点红，

解寄无边春！

注释

　　①鄢陵：即今河南鄢陵县。②王主簿：生平不可考。③折枝：花卉
画的一种表现手法，只画连枝折下来的部分。

Flowering Branches Written on Paintings by Secretary Wang of Yanling

I

To overstress resemblance of form
In painting is a childish view.
Who thinks in verse there is a norm,
To poetry he's got no clew.
In painting as in poetry,
We like what's natural and new.
Bian Luan painted birds vividly;
Zhao Chang's flowers to nature were true.
But these two pictures surpass them:
They're fairer and more elaborate.
We won't believe from a red stem
The beauty of spring can radiate.

二

瘦竹如幽人，
幽花如处女。
低昂枝上雀，
摇荡花间雨。
双翎决将起，
众叶纷自举。
可怜采花蜂，
清蜜寄两股。
若人富天巧，
春色入毫楮。
悬知君能诗，
寄声求妙语。

II

Slender bamboos look like recluse;

Like maidens blossom lonely flowers.

Birds bend the branch which they let loose,

And shaken flowers fall in showers.

They flap their wings and up they fly,

And stir all the leaves of the trees.

With nectar gathered on the thigh,

Busy are the laborious bees.

This painter has a gift for art,

His brush preserves the beauty of spring.

I think he is a poet at heart,

And wait for a reply this verse will bring.

赏析

  第一首诗抒写诗人对于"形似"论的意见。第二首表现作者愿意听到王主簿对写诗作画的"妙语"。这组诗是用诗歌形式评论文艺作品的名篇，其中关于"形似"的见解颇受后人注目。[1]

---

1 缪钺等：《宋诗鉴赏辞典》，上海辞书出版社1987年版，第434—436页。

赠刘景文①

荷尽已无擎雨盖，

菊残犹有傲霜枝。

一年好景君须记：

最是橙黄橘绿时。

注释

　　①刘景文：即刘季孙，字景文，时任两浙兵马都监，驻杭州。苏轼视他为国士，曾上表推荐。

To Liu Jingwen

Lotuses put up no umbrellas to the rain;

Yet frost-proof branches of chrysanthemum remain.

Do not forget of a year the loveliest scene:

When oranges are yellow and tangerines are green.

赏析

　　本诗前两句写傲雪凌霜的气节，后两句勉励朋友乐观向上，抒发了作者的广阔胸襟和对友人的支持，托物言志，意境高远。[1]

1　孙凡礼、刘尚荣：《苏轼诗词选》，中华书局2005年版，第176—177页。

上元侍饮楼上三首呈同列三首选一

澹月疏星绕建章^①，

仙风吹下御炉香。

侍臣鹄立^②通明殿，

一朵红云^③捧玉皇^④。

注释

①建章：即建章宫。②鹄立：像天鹅般引颈直立。③红云：比喻穿红袍的侍臣。④玉皇：指宋帝。

Royal Banquet on Lantern Festival

The morning moon and stars shed light on palace hall;

Celestial breeze spreads royal incense over all.

The ministers attend the banquet like cranes proud,

The emperor seems to reign from the rosy cloud.

赏析

　　本诗为元宵夜皇帝举行宴会而群臣陪饮的所见所感。此诗虽写颂扬皇家之辞，但十分得体，有君臣之仪，无阿谀之意。全诗设境肃穆隆重，明朗壮美，语言自然而形象，如身临其境，见证了宋王朝升平时期的一次皇家盛典。[1]

1　蒙万夫、阎琦主编:《千家诗鉴赏辞典》，陕西人民教育出版社1991年版，第24—26页。

儋州：此生归路愈茫然

慈湖夹①阻风五首选三

一

捍索②桅竿立啸空，

篙师酣寝浪花中。

故应菅蒯③知心腹，

弱缆能争万里风。

二

此生归路愈茫然，

无数青山水拍天。

犹有小船来卖饼，

喜闻墟落在山前。

注释

　　①慈湖夹：在今安徽当涂县北。②捍索：船桅两旁的索。③菅（jiān）蒯（kuǎi）：草绳。

Held up by Head Winds on the Gorge of the Kind Lake

I

The mast with stretched ropes stands sighing in the air,
The punter soundly sleeps by the white-crested waves.
You should repose your trust in these hemp ropes, howe'er:
Weak as they seem, they can stand a strong wind which raves.

II

When can I come back to my hometown? I'm at a loss.
Beyond countless blue hills waves rise into the sky.
As cakes are sold in a small boat we come across,
We are glad to find there is a village nearby.

三

卧看落月横千丈，

起唤清风得半帆。

且并水村欹侧过，

人间何处不巉岩①！

注释

　　①巉（chán）岩：山石险峻。这里借喻人生道路的难行。

III

Abed, I see the setting moon shine far and wide;

Rising, I call the wind and it fills half the sail.

Let us go round the village by the waterside.

How can we in our life encounter no adverse gale?

赏析 这组七绝描写作者贬谪途中的自然景色和生活情景。小诗寓哲理于形象之中，借助日常景物表现作者直面现实，不避艰险，随遇而安的人生态度。

纵笔

白头萧散①满霜风②，

小阁藤床寄病容。

报道先生春睡美，

道人轻打五更钟。

注释

①萧散：萧疏冷落的样子。这里形容头发稀少。②霜风：形容头发披离。

An Impromptu Verse Written in Exile

Dishevelled white hair flows in the wind like frost spread,

In my small study I lie ill in a wicker bed.

Knowing that I am sleeping a sweet sleep in spring,

The Taoist priest takes care morning bells softly ring.

赏析

　　本诗为苏轼贬居惠州时的诗作，表现出他与当地人融洽相处的友好关系，也体现了苏轼随遇而安的性格。[1]

1　陈迩冬：《苏东坡诗词选》，人民文学出版社1982年版，第82—83页。

被酒①独行，遍至子云、威、徽、先觉四黎②之舍三首 选二

一

半醒半醉问诸黎，

竹刺藤梢步步迷。

但寻牛矢③觅归路，

家在牛栏西复西。

二

总角④黎家三小童，

口吹葱叶⑤送迎翁。

莫作天涯万里意，

溪边自有舞雩风⑥。

注释

　　①被酒：刚喝过酒。②四黎：子云、威、徽、先觉都是海南黎族人，姓黎，故称"四黎"。③牛矢：牛粪。④总角：儿童把头发扎成髻，借指幼年。⑤口吹葱叶：吹葱是一种儿童游戏。⑥舞雩（yú）风：祈雨舞蹈的土著民风。

Drunken, I Walk Alone to Visit the Four Lis

I

Half drunk, half sober, I ask my way to the four Lis,

Bamboo spikes and rattan creepers tangle before me.

I can but follow the way where cow turds are spread,

And find their houses farther west of cattle shed.

II

Three or four children of the Lis with their hair tressed,

Blowing green onion pipes, welcome me the old guest.

Do not seek happiness to the end of the earth!

By the side of the brook you'll find genuine mirth.

赏析

这组诗把朴素内容写得生动而富有风趣，于毫不经意间呈现出行云流水般的活泼姿态，彰显出大家气格。

纵笔三首选一

寂寂东坡一病翁，
白须萧散满霜风。
小儿误喜朱颜在，
一笑那知是酒红！

An Impromptu Verse Written by the Seaside

The lonely Master of Eastern Slope lies ill in bed,
Dishevelled white hair flows in the wind like frost spread.
Seeing my crimson face, my son is glad I'm fine,
I laugh for he does not know that I have drunk wine.

注释

　　苏轼作此诗时已 64 岁，且病魔缠身，正处于"食无肉，居无室，病无药，出无友"的困境。诗中情绪的变化、色彩的变化、反复的否定和肯定，体现出诗人过人的胸襟和笔力。[1]

1　韩林元：《历代名人谪琼诗选注》，河南大学出版社1990年版，第20—21页。

澄迈驿①通潮阁二首

一

倦客愁闻归路遥，

眼明飞阁俯长桥。

贪观白鹭横秋浦，

不觉青林没晚潮。

二

余生欲老海南村，

帝遣巫阳招我魂。

杳杳②天低鹘③没处，

青山一发是中原。

注释

    ①澄迈驿：设在澄迈县（今海南省北部）的驿站。②杳杳：无影无声。
③鹘：一种鸟鹰。

The Tide Pavilion at Chengmai Post

I

A tired wayfarer's sad his home is far away,
Seeing a pavilion o'er a bridge on his way.
I admire white egrets crossing autumn riverside,
Unaware the green woods are drowned in evening tide.

II

I'd end my life in the village by the South Sea,
The Celestial Court sends a witch to recall me.
Far, far away birds vanish into the low skies,
Beyond a stretch of blue hills the Central Plain lies.

赏析

第一首描绘登通潮阁所见情景，第二首化用典故抒发浓烈的思乡之情。两首诗充分体现了苏诗"清雄"的风格特点。[1]

1 　缪钺等：《宋诗鉴赏辞典》，上海辞书出版社1987年版，第464—465页。

过岭

七年来往^①我何堪！

又试曹溪^②一勺甘。

梦里似曾迁海外，

醉中不觉到江南。

波生濯足鸣空涧，

雾绕征衣滴翠岚。

谁遣山鸡忽惊起，

半岩花雨落毵毵^③。

注释

①七年来往：苏轼从被贬惠州到回虔州，共计七年。②曹溪：在广东曲江东南。③毵（sān）毵：毛发、枝条等细长垂拂、纷披散乱的样子，这里形容落花如雨。

Passing the Ridge

How could I bear journeys to and fro for seven years!
Again I taste sweet water in the Crooked Stream.
With drunken eyes I see the Southern land appears;
My exile by the seaside seems but like a dream.
Waves roaring in the gully can still wash my feet;
Mist dripping like green drops moistens a wayfarer's frock.
As I pass by, a pheasant startled flies so fleet
That flowers fall in showers over half the rock.

赏析

  本诗是苏轼北归途中经过大庾岭所作的一首诗。该诗抒发了诗人对自己曲折坎坷人生的无限感慨之情。

归朝欢
和苏坚伯固①

我梦扁舟浮震泽②，

雪浪摇空千顷白。

觉来满眼是庐山，

倚天无数开青壁。

此生长接淅③，

与君同是江南客。

梦中游，

觉来清赏，

同作飞梭掷。

注释

①伯固：即苏坚，曾任杭州临税官，是苏轼的得力助手。②震泽：太湖古称震泽。③接淅：指匆匆忙忙。

Happy Return to the Court
In Reply to Su Jian

I dream my leaflike boat on the vast lake afloat,
Snowlike waves surge up for miles and whiten the air.
I wake to find Mount Lu resplendent to my eye,
Blue cliffs upon blue cliffs open against the sky.
I've suffered setbacks all my life long;
You and I sing alike the roamer's song.
Dreaming of boating on the lake,
I like the thrilling scene when awake,
And feel as happy as the shuttle flies.

明日西风还挂席①，

唱我新词泪沾臆②。

灵均③去后楚山空，

澧阳④兰芷无颜色。

君才如梦得⑤，

武陵⑥更在西南极。

《竹枝词》，

莫摇⑦新唱，

谁谓古今隔？

注释

　　①挂席：犹挂帆。②沾臆：泪水浸湿胸前。③灵均：屈原的字。
④澧阳：今湖南澧县。⑤梦得：唐代诗人刘禹锡，字梦得。⑥武陵：今
湖南常德一带。⑦莫摇：少数民族名称。

You will set sail in western breeze tomorrow;

I'll croon in tears for you a new verse full of sorrow.

When Poet Qu is gone, the Southern Mountain's bare.

Sweet orchids and clovers will lose their hue

Like the poet of Willow Branch Song, you

Will go farther southwest.

But you may compose as a guest.

And then who says

The modern age cannot surpass the bygone days?

赏析

　　本词上片写作者与伯固同游庐山的所见所感，下片另起一意，写对伯固的勉励。全词以雄健的笔调，营造出纯真爽朗、境界阔达、气度昂扬的词境，抒写了作者的浩逸襟怀。[1]

1　　王水照、朱刚：《苏轼诗词文选评》，上海古籍出版社2004年版，第70—71页。

蝶恋花
春景

花褪残红青杏小。
燕子飞时，
绿水人家绕。
枝上柳绵吹又少。
天涯何处无芳草！

墙里秋千墙外道。
墙外行人，
墙里佳人笑。
笑渐不闻声渐悄。
多情却被无情恼。

Butterfly in Love with Flower
Red Flowers Fade

Red flowers fade and green apricots are still small

When swallows pass

Over blue water which surrounds the garden wall.

Most willow catkins have been blown away, alas!

But there is no place where will not grow sweet green grass.

Without the wall there's a path within there's a swing.

A passer-by

Hears the fair maiden's laughter in the garden ring.

As the ringing laughter dies away by and by,

For the enchantress the enchant'd can only sigh.

赏析

    本词上阕写春光易逝带来的伤感，下阕写得遇佳人却无缘一晤，展现了词人对春光流逝的叹息，以及自己的情感不为人知的烦恼。全词词意婉转，于清新中蕴含哀怨，意境朦胧，韵味无穷。[1]

---

1   王思宇：《苏轼词赏析集》，巴蜀书社1996年版，第313—315页。

西江月
梅花

玉骨①那愁瘴雾②？

冰姿③自有仙风。

海仙时遣探芳丛，

倒挂绿毛幺凤④。

素面常嫌粉涴⑤，

洗妆不褪唇红⑥。

高情⑦已逐晓云空，

不与梨花同梦。

注释

　　①玉骨：梅花枝干的美称。②瘴雾：南方山林中的湿热之气。③冰姿：淡雅的姿态。④绿毛幺凤：岭南的一种珍禽，似鹦鹉。⑤涴（wò）：沾污。⑥唇红：喻红色的梅花。⑦高情：高隐超然物外之情。

The Moon on the West River
To the Fairy of Mume Flower

Your bones of jade defy miasmal death;
Your flesh of snow exhales immortal breath.
The sea sprite among flowers often sends to you
A golden-eyed, green-feathered cockatoo.

Powder would spoil your face;
Your lips need no rouge cream.
As high as morning cloud you rise with grace;
With pear flower you won't share your dream.

赏析

　　本词是苏轼为悼念随自己贬谪惠州的侍妾朝云而作。上阕写惠州梅花的风姿、神韵，下阕追写梅花的形貌。全词境象朦胧虚幻，情韵悠长，为苏轼婉约词中的佳作。[1]

1　唐圭璋等：《唐宋词鉴赏辞典（唐·五代·北宋）》，上海辞书出版社1988年版，第630—633页。